CHOKING GAP

Luther Hayes is plenty sore at Daco Ward for giving the evidence that put him behind bars for fifteen years. When he is sprung from jail, he goes looking for Daco to settle the score — but failing to find him, he shoots Daco's wife instead. Prepared to follow Hayes all the way to hell to get his revenge, Daco's trail is hard and long. But a partnership with big Tondu Adams lightens the load, and the pair are soon on course to drag Hayes to justice . . .

JOSEPH JOHN McGRAW

CHOKING GAP

Complete and Unabridged

LINFORD
Leicester

First published in Great Britain in 2012 by
Robert Hale Limited
London

First Linford Edition
published 2014
by arrangement with
Robert Hale Limited
London

A catalogue record for this book is available
from the British Library.

ISBN 978–1–4448–1997–7

Published by
F. A. Thorpe (Publishing)
Anstey, Leicestershire

Set by Words & Graphics Ltd.
Anstey, Leicestershire
Printed and bound in Great Britain by
T. J. International Ltd., Padstow, Cornwall

This book is printed on acid-free paper

To JJC, the real McGraw

1

Just before the bell for noontime chow was rung, the main gates were blown and shots were fired.

Major Frank Pilling, governor of Maynor County Military Prison, leaped out of his chair, scattering the papers on his desk, and rushed to the window of his office. Both gates had been blasted wide open. One hung drunkenly on its hinges and the other was lying flat on the ground where it had been flung by the force of the explosion. Through the clearing smoke rode a dozen mounted men whooping and exchanging shots with the prison guards. Major Tilling swore. Then, buckling on his gun-belt, he ran outside and started barking orders.

His men, caught unawares, put up little resistance. Most were unarmed, being on routine, not guard duties. They dived for cover. The intruders followed them and cut six or eight down each with a bullet in the back. Withering fire raked the main block where the hard cases were locked up. Meeting little or no resistance in return, the gunmen abandoned their horses, which ran this way and that in a panic. It took no more than two shakes of a lamb's tail to shoot the main door open. The attackers piled inside. Barrels of guns appeared at the windows and kept up a steady stream of fire, which forced the guards outside to keep their heads down.

One shot caught Major Pilling in the shoulder. He staggered under the impact and fell back through the door he'd just come out of.

Then there was silence before the defenders, stunned by the suddenness of the attack, started firing back at the front of the cell-block. The shooting grew sporadic. The soldiers kept their heads down and offered few targets, but they had nothing to shoot at either, except blank windows, walls and the closed door of the cell-block.

Inside, a short, square-shouldered man named Zeke Goodwin held his six-shooter against the throat of Duty Sergeant Ernest Warner and told him to hand over the keys to the cells. Somewhere along one of the three corridors leading off from the guard-room a voice was yelling. Zeke recognized it at once.

'Is he still in the same cell?' he barked at the duty officer.

'Who you talking about?' said Sergeant Warner.

'Hayes, Luther Hayes.'

'Now there's one real bad man,' said the sergeant.

'Never mind the character reference; let him out.'

'I know you,' said the sergeant. 'Goodwin. Released last month.'

'And enjoyed every minute of it since. Now put your gun on the desk, nice and easy, stop talking and do like I say.'

Left with no choice, the sergeant, careful not to make any sudden movements, eased his gun from its holster, placed it on his desk, raised his arms and began walking down the middle of the three corridors. Goodwin and two others followed. As they passed the cells lining both sides, the occupants hollered and whistled encouragement, for they too knew Zeke Goodwin. But Zeke paid them no heed and did not, as they urged, stop to unlock their cell doors and let them out. With his gun in the sergeant's back, the procession walked to the end of the corridor.

Luther Hayes was sitting on the edge of his bunk. He was not alone. Jed Purdue was standing in the middle of the cell they shared.

Luther was a big man, barrel-chested and tall. The thick, muscular forearms which stuck out of the sleeves of his check shirt ended in a pair of fists as tough as seasoned oak. They were square; the knuckles had been flattened by the heavy punches they'd landed. His hair was grizzled, for he was no longer a young man. He had served fifteen of a thirty-year sentence and his beard had turned grey, probably as a way of passing the time. When he saw Zeke, he stood up.

'What took you so long?' he snarled.

'Arrangements to make,' said Zeke briefly, digging his gun hard into the sergeant's back as a way of ordering him to unlock the door.

Then Luther was outside, in the corridor. He breathed deeply, inhaling his freedom, and smashed a fist into the sergeant's face. There was a sound of breaking bone.

'Quit that,' snapped Zeke. 'There ain't time for it.'

'How'd you get in?' asked Luther.

'Wagon with gunpowder, blowed up the gates, rode in through the smoke.'

'How we going to get out?'

But Zeke was too busy to answer. He bent down and relieved Sergeant Warner of his keys. He proceeded to unlock the cell doors and tossed the whole bunch to the last prisoner who took off with them into the next corridor. Soon the place was full of released prisoners crowing and jostling. They broke down the door to the office where the guards had taken refuge.

'Get their guns, boys, and lock 'em up!' cried Zeke above the hullabaloo.

The guards, outnumbered and helpless, were disarmed and pushed roughly into the cells which had just been vacated.

Zeke shot the lock off the arms store and handed out the guns and a few rounds of ammo apiece.

'And now we go!' he cried.

He flung open the door and urged the men he had released through it. With a roar, they raced out, waving their guns and looking for something to shoot at.

Luther and Jed Purdue were about to go after them and join the fun, but Zeke told them to stop. Gathering them and the rest of the attackers around him, he barked:

'Follow me. They're targets for the soldiers. We go this way.'

He led them down the other corridor

which was lined with offices and store-rooms. At the far end was a door. Zeke shot off the lock, opened the door an inch, then another, until he got his head out. He smiled at what he saw.

'We'll give it a coupla minutes, then we go!' he said.

At the front of the building came the sound of yelling and the din of battle. Major Pilling was now on his feet and, nursing his busted shoulder, was giving orders, rallying his men and trying to gain control of the situation. But the prisoners were trained soldiers too and knew how to organize. They put up a decent scrap, making the most of what cover there was. A few of the escapees tried their luck. They caught the terrified horses, which were still running every which way around the drill yard, swung into the saddles and made for the gate, hell for leather. Five gave it a try; two made it and galloped out of sight.

In the end the battle proved to be one-sided. The mutineers were out-numbered and outgunned. One by one, they threw down their guns as their ammo ran out. But it wasn't over yet. Shots were still being fired when there was a loud 'crump!' which came from behind the cell-block.

Responding to the assault on the prison, the guards at the rear had redeployed at the double to reinforce their comrades who were under attack at the front of the compound. When Zeke's second charge of gunpowder blew a large hole in the rear wall, there were no defenders to prevent them walking through it and, once they were outside, from getting on the fresh set of horses which were waiting for them.

Wearing a broad grin, Luther sat in his saddle and felt good.

'Which way now?' he called.

'Follow me!' replied Zeke as he dug his heels into his horse's ribs.

In less than a minute, the space outside the breach in the wall was empty. The dust started to settle. From start to finish, the raid had taken less than twenty minutes.

As the prison surgeon bandaged his shoulder, Major Pilling began preparing himself for the inquiry which would be set up to look into the raid and his handling of it.

He didn't give snuff for his chances.

2

The moment Daco Ward rounded the bluff he knew something was wrong.

The trail had taken him past Wolf Rock and through the pinewoods before bringing him to its highest point at the foot of Cloudy Bluff. From there he could look down on Green Pasture, his very own piece of Ogmore County, bought and paid for at the government rate of a dollar fifty the acre. To raise the money, he'd herded steers, driven a stage, ridden shotgun, guarded cattle, cut timber, even had a stint running a cookshack for Morgan Agricultural Feeds up in Wyoming. He'd made his money the hard, the honest way.

But now the hairs on the back of his neck were standing on end. Something was wrong.

He'd ridden into Blackmill Creek two days back. He had business there.

He needed to look over the horseflesh in Dubois's livery stables to replace a draw horse that had died on him, and file an order at Dyson's Mercantile Store for ironmongery, mainly materials to put right what the winter had done here and there to his fences and cattle pens.

He'd spent the night at Doc McKinley's. Whenever he went to Blackmill Creek, he always stayed with the doc. They'd usually open a bottle and kill it the slow way, yarning over the old days. Whiskey was their drink. They went back a long way. They'd met in the army; the doc had dug a bullet out of Daco's leg and Daco had saved the doc's neck in an ambush. When they ran out of olden days to chew over, they found other things to talk about — the price of bacon, how there'd been too much or too little rain, and when the town would get to see the railways the businessmen were always talking about.

Daco Ward had settled into his life as a small-time cattleman.

After he'd handed over his life savings to Lawyer Timms to clinch the sale of the land, he wasn't far off broke. He had enough cash to buy half-a-dozen head of cattle, which he nursed through his first winter. The next year, his small herd had grown with the birth of three calves. He lived quietly, spent nothing that wasn't strictly needed for growing the herd. Within five years he felt he was set up.

He built a cabin of logs for himself. It was small. His barns were bigger, the difference in size being the measure of the importance he gave to his own comfort against the welfare of his beasts. After a while, he built himself a bigger cabin and invited neighbours to the house-warming. He was well liked. Knowing him for a bachelor, the ladies baked pies and brought cooked meats and lemonade and home-brewed beer. They were a good crowd. His nearest neighbours Ed Jepson and his wife Stella came, but Doc McKinley who brought his daughter, Virginia, were the first he invited. How could it not be so? The doc was the reason he'd come to Ogmore County in the first place. When the War was over, they'd kept in touch and Daco, being by his own admission a drifter with no roots, made a bee-line for his old friend's town the minute he thought he'd got together enough cash to start up his cattle-raising scheme.

Ginny McKinley had been twelve and pretty when Daco arrived. Eight years later she was a beauty. With the doc's blessing they were wed and now, half-a-dozen years later, Daco had a boy they'd named Tom. Knowing Ginny and Tom depended on him strengthened his determination to make a success of what he had begun.

He sat on his horse and looked down into the valley. A stream ran through the middle of it. The land on either side was neatly divided up by fences and in the pastures, cattle grazed. But they were not happy.

The cows were in distress because

they hadn't been milked. They lowed and stood still in ways that were not natural.

On the far side of the stream were the barns and the cabin Daco had built. There was no sign of life inside or outside the barns and the house seemed deserted. He couldn't see Ginny or Tom or Burr, the mutt that went everywhere he did. There was no smoke at the chimney. Nothing moved except the branches in the breeze.

His first impulse was to dig his spurs in his horse's sides and get down there to find out what was wrong.

But he hadn't been a soldier for nothing. Before he moved, he wanted to know if there were any unpleasant surprises waiting for him. He scoured the valley sides systematically, then the banks of the stream and the farm buildings. Nothing moved. The sun glinted on no rifle barrels. Keeping a careful eye open, he nudged his horse forward. Faint hoof marks showed on the trail. It looked like a group of riders, too many to say for sure, had gone down to the farm. The tracks had been blurred by a day and a night of wind and told him little. But no return tracks showed, so the riders had not come back the way they'd arrived. Could be they were still there. But finding nothing suspicious, he continued on his way. When the cattle saw him, they moved in his direction. With growing confidence he ignored them and went straight on to the cabin.

He wished he had a gun. It was years since he'd worn one — the life he led didn't call for guns.

The door was open. His senses on full alert, he paused briefly then stepped inside. After the bright sunlight, it took a moment for his eyes to adjust. He didn't need that long to smell the trace of cheroot smoke. Ginny hated cheroots and no one had smoked any in his house since the day of the house-warming. He saw dirty glasses on a side table; there were the remnants of a meal in the kitchen. Whoever had eaten it sure were messy eaters. They weren't the sort who'd smarten up their manners just because Ginny told them to. They weren't the sort either who washed dishes. Ginny's kitchen was a mess.

The ashes in the stove were cold.

Daco wasn't liking any part of what he saw. But all the same, he called her name.

'Ginny? You home, sweetheart?'

She didn't answer but he heard a faint cry.

'Pa? Is that you?'

'Where are you, Tom?'

'The men locked me in the wood store.'

Daco ran outside and round to the side of the cabin where he had built a rough lean-to, which kept his burning wood dry. A length of squared-off half-planed timber had been jammed against the door to hold it shut. He yanked it free and let Tom out. Tom was nearly six. He threw his arms around his father's knees and clung to him.

16

Daco took him inside and gave him a cup of water, for the boy was thirsty. It was no good asking how long he'd been locked up because Tom was too young to know. Daco found him something to eat, a piece of his ma's cake and a couple of spoonfuls of jam, and slowly calmed the boy down. Gradually, Daco pieced together what had happened.

Tom had been playing on the stoop with Burr when he saw three riders approaching.

'What did they want?'

'They asked if you lived here.'

'They knew my name?' said Daco in surprise. All the folks in Ogmore County knew where he lived and wouldn't need to ask. As to strangers, none ever just stopped by.

'Burr, he didn't like one of the men. When he barked and showed his teeth, the man kicked him so hard he ran away howling.'

'That wasn't very friendly, Tom. What did the men do next?'

'Ma came out to see what all the fuss

17

was. Then she told me to go and find Burr and play with him down by the stream.'

Tom did what he was told. He couldn't remember how long he stayed by the stream throwing a stick for Burr to fish out of the water. After a while, he felt hungry and went back to the cabin to get a biscuit from his ma. But the men had tied her to a chair. There was blood on her face.

Daco clenched his fists. He kept his voice as calm as he could make it.

'Was she all right? Apart from the blood on her face?'

'Think so. But she couldn't get me a biscuit.

'What happened next?'

'One of the men, not the one who kicked Burr, but another one, this one was the chief, he told me to show him where the biscuits were kept. He took the tin and started eating them himself. He didn't give me one.'

It took Daco a good ten minutes to put the next part together. Not getting his biscuit, Tom went back outside again, so he didn't see what happened in the kitchen. Somehow, Ginny had got free (or maybe they'd untied her for reasons he could only guess) and grabbed a knife. Tom heard shouting and then his ma had come running out of the cabin real fast. She still had the knife in her hand. Tom saw red on the blade. A man with blood on his hand came out after her. The man who'd eaten the biscuits appeared in the doorway and shouted for her to stop. When she didn't, he took out his gun, aimed and fired. She fell down in tall grass near the furthest cow byre.

Holding Tom by the hand, Daco walked to the place. Sure enough, there she was. The tall grass swayed over her and cast delicate shadows over her back and the red hole through which her life blood had oozed away.

'Is she going to be all right, Pa?'

Daco shook his head. The shock of it left despair and grief and finally outrage. In a tight voice, he said:

'No, Tom, she won't.'

They walked back to the cabin. The first thing to do was prepare a place for her to lay until what were commonly called 'arrangements' could be made.

Tom interrupted his thoughts.

'After that, they locked me in the wood store. Before they shut the door, one of the men, the one with the blood on his hand, said to give you this paper.'

The paper was thin, like the torn-out flyleaf of a Bible. On it were words in rough pencil — they had been scratched rather than written. The words were just names.

The names were: 'Luther Hayes, Zeke Goodwin, Jed Purdue.'

Good wishes had not been added.

3

It all went back to a time, years before, when Daco had been wet behind the ears. He'd signed up for the War on the side of the Yankee states, which were going to teach the slavers of the Confederacy to mend their ways. The War had made a man of him, if that phrase meant learning to look with the eyes in the back of his head and take no man's word for anything until it was checked out. He'd also learned to shoot straight, drink whiskey, cheat at cards and never volunteer.

He never quite got the hang of that last requirement. Because he believed in the cause he was fighting for, he was willing to put his shoulder to whatever wheel needed turning and always pushed as hard as he could. He despised those who didn't. And chief among the shirkers was Corporal Luther Hayes.

Hayes was a big man with a big mouth. He had big hands too and he used them if any man crossed him, whatever his size. Daco had seen him batter recruits half his weight to a pulp and even beat much larger opponents with a longer reach and handy fists into bloody submission. Officers commanding the regiment wanted their men to fight the enemy, not each other. They were furious when they saw their units thinned by the number of hospital cases Luther made for them. If they'd had more born leaders — for Luther was certainly that — they'd have busted him to private. So he kept his rank. Even so, he probably spent more time in irons than any other serving soldier in the War. Luther did not mind. It suited him. He was happier sitting far from the action playing cards with his jailors than risking his neck in a fight he didn't regard as any of his business and for which he had signed up only because he'd been good and drunk at the time.

For some reason, call it the attraction

of opposites, he took a shine to Daco. He added him to his group which already included Jed Purdue and Zeke Goodwin. He showed Daco how to fight dirty and taught him never to back down. Facing up to a man, he said, even if he was bigger than you, was half the battle. It rattled your opponent, made him unsure, and that gave you an opening, an edge.

Jed and Zeke followed him around, fawned on him and ran his errands. But they too were nasty pieces of work. They bullied the other men, promising that Luther would do them over if they didn't do what they were told. This usually meant handing over part of their pay or tobacco or any grub they were sent from home.

Daco was never a fully paid-up member of Luther's club of bravos. But he knew that once a man was in, getting out was hard to do. He had seen what happened to men who tried it. The lucky ones ended up in hospital. For the unlucky ones, hospital was too late.

Then Daco had been made up to sergeant.

Luther was vastly amused and gave his promotion a whiskey-soaked welcome. It didn't bother him that he was now outranked, for no one, not even generals, gave orders to Luther Hayes. Quite the opposite: he got to thinking that having a sergeant on side had its advantages. He told Daco to keep his ears open and let him know if anything big was being planned, especially shipments of military supplies which could be diverted and sold or squirrelled away where they could be retrieved after the War, whichever side won. He already had a racket going on the side, selling sacks of army flour and sides of army beef to civilians. He also got his hands on ammo, guns and any sort of equipment and was not particular who he sold them to. He had particularly close contacts with equally crooked counterparts in the Confederate ranks.

War was good for Luther. He would

hear nothing said against it.

But Daco finally snapped. What did it started with an order from the officer of the day. Lieutenant Adams had come fresh to the unit and knew nothing of Luther's record. During an engagement when the regiment had been ordered to hold a position on Powder Ridge and hold off a superior Confederate force, men were needed to re-supply the front-line with ammunition and supplies. Daco was already there on the ridge with his unit. In his absence, Corporal Hayes was next in line to lead the group detailed to carry the ammo. The situation was getting desperate.

Luther jerked to attention and saluted briskly. The ammo was loaded on mules and he and his men set off with it.

After a mile or so, Luther found a hollow in the ground where he and the mules wouldn't be seen and told his boys to stand down. They dug a hole, dumped the heavy boxes in it and covered them with earth. Then they sat down to wait. While they waited, they smoked and jawed. The plan was to return to base saying they couldn't get through because they'd come under intense enemy fire. To save their skins, they'd abandoned the ammo. Later it would be retrieved and sold on. Luther had got away with worse. Luther could be a plausible man.

Daco's unit, on the Yankees' left flank, had come under withering fire. When they were almost out of ammo, he had no choice but to withdraw his men and fight another day. The way back led them through the hollow where Luther and his men had hidden up. When Daco realized that he'd been forced to retreat having lost comrades who hadn't been able to shoot back, he saw red. He ordered his men to arrest Luther and his gang of thieves and reported immediately to Lieutenant Adams, who was a fair-minded man. He questioned Luther, who was quick-tongued enough to get away with it: he could be a very plausible man. But all the brains he was born with were in his fists. Instead of denying the charge or muddying the waters he tried to bribe the lieutenant. He was sent to the calaboose and then taken to a secure military prison well behind the lines. He did not go alone. He implicated Jed Perdue, Zeke Goodwin, Frankie Mason and a number of others. In due course, they all faced a court martial. They were accused of treason under fire, but Luther — plausibly — claimed they had buried the ammo to prevent it getting into enemy hands. He created enough doubt to persuade the court to settle for a conviction for profiteering, based on his track record and Daco's evidence. He was sentenced to thirty years' hard labour and Jed and Zeke to fifteen apiece.

And now Luther was back. Maybe he'd talked his way out of jail or been sprung. Either way, he was in a mood to settle old scores. He'd had twenty years to think about Daco, the man who had sold him down the river.

Daco thought Luther must have traced him through army records.

Leading a gang of desperadoes, flanked by Zeke and Jed, with a gun in his belt, a horse to ride and a trail to follow, Luther was in control again.

Before he hit the trail that led to Ogmore County, he got him a stake.

By that time, rustling a driven herd of beef was no longer the style. It was hard work, took a gang of men to do it and afterwards the rustlers were left with a herd on their hands. Driving steers was heavy toil and selling them was not easy. Buyers wouldn't touch animals with brands they knew and were likely to inform the law, which was now better organized than in the old pioneering days. No, Luther did it the new way. He hung around towns where the herds were bought and sold, followed the vendors and saw which put their money in banks and which stuffed gold or cash in their saddle-bags. After they'd paid off their drivers, the cattlemen would head home accompanied by just a few of their regular hands. Luther chose his moment and took their money and, to be on the safe side, their lives.

He believed what people said about dead men telling no tales.

He also believed it applied to women.

4

There was a good turnout in Blackmill Creek for Ginny's funeral. She and Daco were well liked. But many were also obligated to Doc McKinley for services which cannot be paid for with dollar bills. Paying their respects went some way to settling their dues. Ginny was laid to rest under a line of young cypresses. She would have liked that.

After the service, Sheriff Bannen came up to Daco.

'I've had men out looking, but nobody's seen hide nor hair of those men. But we found some tracks. They were old but the best guess is that there were around a dozen of 'em. They're long gone, Daco, and they won't be back. Not after what they done to Ginny.'

Daco didn't argue and thanked him for the trouble he'd taken. But he knew

30

Luther; he'd be back. Daco was the one he wanted. Ginny had just got in the way.

He told the doc he couldn't sit on his hands and do nothing about the men who'd murdered his sweet Ginny. He couldn't live with that.

'So I'm going after them,' he said. 'But I'll need your help.'

'You sure about this?' asked the doc doubtfully. 'I've lived longer than you and I've learned that bad things happen. There's no rhyme nor reason to it. When bad things happen to a man, sometimes that man would be wise just to let it go. If he don't, the bitterness will eat into his heart and he'll never be free of it. Besides, what about Tom? Surely you're not thinking of taking him with you?'

'That's where I need your help. Look, Doc, you may be right about letting things go, but it won't do in this case. You don't know Luther Hayes. He figures I was the one that landed him with a thirty-year sentence . . . '

31

'But that's ridiculous,' said the doc. 'He got himself into trouble because he's a crook.'

'Yes, but Luther don't see it that way. He'll be back and he won't be satisfied until I'm a notch on the butt of his gun. And meantime, if Tom was to get in his way — '

'Sheriff Bannen's a good man. He'll look out for Luther and his gang.'

'Doc, they're killers. They're jay-hawkers who've been marauding ever since the War ended. It would take more than Bannen and his deputies to stop Hayes and his cut-throats.'

'Very well,' said the doc after a moment. 'How can I help?'

'Look, Doc, I got to do this, otherwise I'll spend the rest of my life looking over my shoulder. And looking out for Tom too, not to mention you and everyone else I know. So I'm asking: will you look after the boy, wipe his nose, raise him until I get back?'

'Of course. Be glad to, son.'

And so it was fixed.

Daco also fixed it with Ed Jepson to take his steers back to his range and graze them there. Once he'd collected them, on no account was Ed to go anywhere near Daco's place. Hayes might show up at any time.

At Dubois's livery stables, he picked out a chestnut mustang and paid for it with the flatboard wagon which he wouldn't be needing now. At Dyson's Mercantile, he equipped himself with a .44 Winchester, a six-gun for his hip and a hunting knife to hang on his belt. He also bought a bedroll, a cookpan and a tin drinking mug.

He said goodbye to the doc and told Tom to be good. Then he pulled himself up into his saddle and rode out of town.

When he reached the foot of Cloudy Bluff, he reined in his horse and looked down on his pastures.

Ed Jepson had already come for his cows for the fields were empty. But there were signs of life. A dozen horses were tethered in back of his house and there was smoke coming out of his chimney.

He dismounted and tied the mustang to a branch of a tree growing just off the trail, out of sight. He took the Winchester from the saddle holster and checked his Colt. Then, keeping his head well down, he started moving cautiously down the slope.

Bushes and boulders gave him good cover that took him to within thirty yards of his front door. He crouched behind a rock and waited.

From the cabin he had built came raucous laughter and then the sound of angry voices. All of a sudden, a man Daco had never seen before, small-made, wiry and with a bald head, came crashing backwards through the door and landed on the seat of his pants in the dust. He stood up, shook his head and wiped the blood off his chin. Then he headed back for the cabin. He clearly hadn't had enough and was going to finish what had been started.

He had one foot on the stoop when a

shot sang out from somewhere to Daco's right.

The bald man was stopped in mid-step. He clutched one leg, toppled then fell flat on his face.

He didn't move. He didn't want to get shot again.

The voices inside went quiet. Daco saw Ginny's kitchen curtain twitch. There was another shot which was followed by a howl of pain and then a volley of shots came from every window in the cabin.

Daco kept his head down.

Someone shouted an order and the firing ceased as abruptly as it had begun. The unseen sniper loosed off another shot. The response was a second hail of bullets, none of which hit any target. Again there was the order to stop shooting. He smiled approvingly at the hidden sharpshooters' tactics. At this rate, the men in his house would soon be low on ammo.

He waited to see what would happen next.

In the sudden silence, he heard the click of a latch, which he recognized as belonging to his back door. The squatters also had a plan. They were sending men out who, using the cover which was as good at the back as at the front, could circle the cabin and flush their attacker out into the open.

It was time to get back to the trail. He didn't want to get caught in the trap. Besides, he'd have a better view from there.

Daco returned the way he had come. He climbed easily and silently and was no more than twenty yards from his regular vantage point under the Bluff when he heard the scrunch of a boot on gravel behind him and to his left. It was close. He froze but was too late. The barrel of a gun was suddenly pressed against his ear.

'Make one move and you're dead!'

A large hand reached for his six-gun and eased it out of its holster. Both men remained without moving. Then the pressure of the gun slackened and Daco felt his captor relax. But they remained as they were. Voices from the valley below floated up to them.

'Lou's hurt. Anyone else get shot?'

'The sniper was here!' someone called. 'I found prints.'

'There's no sign of him! He's gone!'

'Maybe. Any tracks worth following?'

'I want that shooter!' cried a thunderous voice, which could only have belonged to Luther.

The man with the gun growled into Daco's ear: 'They'll be on my trail soon. I'd have killed you before this, but a shot would have brought them running. I've not got time to waste so tell me who you are and what you're doing here.'

'That's my cabin down there.'

The man relaxed more.

'Those men killed my wife. It's not something I can let lie.'

'Well, mister, if you're intending to go after those men, you got to act smarter. I took you easy. If I'd been one of them, you'd have handed back your dinner pail by now.'

The shooter put his gun away and stood up. He held out Daco's six-gun.

'Here, take it. I reckon we're on the same side. Come on, we got to get out of here.'

He was big, six-three at least, with broad shoulders, narrow hips, and hefty, square fists. Grey eyes looked out frankly over a straight nose and a solid, iron jaw.

When they were mounted up, the man said:

'You know the terrain, it's your patch. Is there a place where we could lie up and keep an eye on them without being seen? I don't want to lose touch with those jayhawkers.'

Daco led the way along a hidden animal trail, which brought them out on a ledge a hundred feet up the face of Cloudy Bluff. From there they had a clear view of the valley. Smoke still snaked up from the chimney but otherwise all was quiet. Daco sat on a rock, pulled out a pouch and rolled a couple of smokes. The man took the one offered, then, inhaling deeply, said:

'All right, give me the full story.'

Instead of complying, Daco looked him in the eye for the first time.

'Don't I know you?' he said.

And then he remembered.

'You're Lieutenant Adams, Philadelphia All-Celtic Infantry, right?'

The man raised a quizzical eyebrow.

'I might be. But who the hell are you?'

'Sergeant Daco Ward. I served under you at Powder Ridge.'

'Well ain't that the darndest thing! I recollect you now, Sergeant. You're the one had the guts to put Luther Hayes on the spot with a charge of stealing ammo. Has that got anything to do with why he's in this neck of the woods?'

'I reckon so. He's plenty sore at me for giving the evidence that got him put in jail for thirty years. He must have got out somehow. Way I see it, he came looking for me and when he couldn't find me, he killed my wife. Shot her in the back. I'll follow him all the way to hell if I have to, but I'll see he gets what's coming to him.'

'I'm sorry to hear your story, Sergeant.'

'And what brings you here, Lieutenant?'

'Captain. I got moved up a rank just before the War ended. After the peace I left the Army and signed up for a marshal. Got me a star to pin on my vest,' he said with a grin. 'After the shooting stopped, a lot of men went to the bad. Couldn't settle to any kind of regular life. I guess they missed the excitement. Some, like Quantrill, were one hundred per cent rotten. They robbed and killed and looted and burned down property and ruined lives. I was one of the men who went looking for such men to bring them to justice. Over time, they nearly all got killed or jailed, so they gave me a desk job. I held off a while. Did other things instead, to fill in the time. I sold patent medicines, taught school, did anything that came along. But I was always broke. So in the end I signed on for their scrivening job. But I never took to it. Me and government paper didn't mix. But four months back, a sheet of it came across my desk which said there'd been a break-out from Maynor County Military Prison. It's a jail for long-term prisoners, the real hard cases. I recognized a few of the names of men who'd escaped. Top of the list was Luther Hayes. The paper also said the escape was set up by Zeke Goodwin and Jed Perdue.'

'How'd he find me?'

'Maybe chance, maybe through army records. There are ways.'

'I'll be sure to ask him before I blow his head off.'

'So I applied to go back to my old job of rounding up marauders. I thought they'd jump at the chance of having a lawman who knew all about Luther and his ways. But they turned me down. Too old, they said. But I was too fired up to go on being a pen-pusher. So I resigned and got on a horse. I picked up their trail and I've been following the Hayes gang for two months. I'm making progress. I got one, maybe two. Lou Prentiss, the guy I winged back there on your stoop, was the third member of Luther's gang that I've removed from the game. I don't shoot 'em dead. I'm no thief-taker, judge, jury and executioner all rolled into one. I just wing them. It's enough. When Luther's men get themselves shot up, he just abandons them, like wounded animals who can't keep up with the pack. Lou is going to have to look out for himself. So the odds are falling. But there's still a lot of them. It's a big job for one man.'

'Are you looking for a partner, Cap?'

'I do believe I am,' said Captain R.G. Adams, late of the Philadelphia All-Celtic Infantry.

5

Below them, there was no sign of activity in the valley, but they heard stray shots that came from under the trees. There were also shouts. Then men came out of the cabin at a crouching run, guns drawn. Luther Hayes was among them. Daco hadn't seen him for fifteen, sixteen years. He'd got heavier but otherwise, as far as Daco could tell from this distance, he looked very much the same, like something out of a bad dream. He was too far away to be worth shooting at. Zeke and Jed were there too and he thought he recognized others, though he couldn't put names to them. But they looked familiar.

'What you reckon Luther will do now?'

'Hard to tell. He's one unpredictable critter but no fool. One thing's for sure, he don't like being stalked. If cornered, he usually takes off. It ain't that he's got no stomach for a fight — the opposite — but fighting's bad for business. He's come a long way to be here. Looks like he's come for you. He missed you once but he can be a patient man. I could be wrong. Maybe he'll go, try again later. But if he stays put, he'll try and find whoever's bothering him.'

'You've been on his trail for a couple of months. What have you got on him?'

'Zeke and one or two others of the original gang served their time and were released half a year ago. Luther and Jed stayed behind bars. Zeke worked the scheme for helping Luther to break out. He's a smart one, but he's no leader. He's Luther's right-hand man. He chooses targets and tells him how to knock them over. They started with about fifteen of them. They're down to a dozen or so. Between them, they've raided trains, robbed banks, held up stage coaches and a lot else besides.'

'Sounds like they've been real busy,'

said Daco. 'They must have made a fortune. What do they spend it on?'

'They whoop it up from time to time, but mostly they keep their pockets closed. They don't want to draw attention to themselves. When the loot is divvied up, Luther gets to keep the lion's share. He must already have put away more money than you or I will ever see.'

'Where's he keep it?'

'Good question. I reckon Luther's got a stash some place.'

'You mean he hides it under a rock that looks like a bear or a wolf to remind him where to find it again?'

'He sure don't keep it in a bank. I reckon he's found a hideaway, like a cave, some place only he and the gang know about.'

He broke off and motioned Daco to be quiet.

Then Daco heard it too, a faint rustling and the occasional snap of a twig under a boot. From time to time the noises stopped. The animal trail they'd used wasn't as hidden as he'd thought and what was coming up it now was no animal.

Luckily, the horses had wandered and were out of sight, grazing on the other side of a bulge in the rock wall. Daco and Captain Adams had just time to flop down among the rocks that littered the ledge and offered some cover. They took out their weapons.

The sounds grew louder and then stopped. Daco saw a low-hanging branch near the mouth of the trail shake. How many of them were there? No sense trying a shot. It wasn't only that he lacked a clear line and a target: a shot would give their position away. And there was no way off the ledge except back down the way they'd come up.

Minutes passed in a silence broken only by the thin, mewing of a pair of buzzards high overhead. The bushes shook again and a man stepped out on to the ledge.

Newt Aldridge! Daco remembered

him from the old days. A mean, low-down, sneaking runt of a man, never looked you in the eye but would stab you in the back given half a chance. How many defenceless people had he gunned down as if he'd been shooting rats? How many lives like his and Ginny's and Tom's had Newt Aldridge ruined? Such men did not deserve to be alive.

It got personal when he saw the bloody bandage he still wore on his hand where Ginny had stuck him.

Before Captain Adams could stop him, Daco was on his feet and running at the intruder. Caught by surprise, Newt was slow to react. He was still snatching for his gun when Daco's first punch smashed into his cheek. Newt dropped his weapon and retreated before the onslaught that followed. A left to the solar plexus brought his head down and a right uppercut whipped it up again and shuffled his brains. A flurry of hooks and jabs took the wind out of him. Soon it was only Daco's punches, delivered with the same cold fury, that kept him on his feet, jerking him up when he started to sag. His face was a mass of cuts and his shirt was red with his own blood. To avoid those terrible, pounding fists, he turned blindly, tripped, staggered and then, with a scream of terror, was suddenly gone.

Breathing heavily, Daco peered over the lip of the ledge.

Newt was lying at the foot of the bluff. He wasn't moving and never would again.

'Where in tarnation did you learn to use your fists like that?' said Captain Adams over his shoulder.

'When I quit the service, I did all sorts of jobs too. I had a stint as a bare-knuckle prize-fighter. I never made the standard, but I learned a few tricks. I know how to defend myself.'

He nodded towards the prone figure a couple of hundred feet below them.

'Newt Aldridge,' he said. 'One for Ginny.'

Then a rifle cracked and took the captain's hat off. Newt's scream had attracted attention; someone was shooting at them from below. They drew back quickly.

'They've spotted us,' said the captain. 'Time to go!'

Daco did not need to be told twice. If they didn't move quickly they'd be caught like butterflies in a net.

'Follow me,' he cried, running to their horses. 'I know this place like the back of my hand.'

He led off down the steep animal track that brought them back on to the trail. By this time, they could hear shouts and the thudding of horses' hoofs coming towards them up the road from the valley.

Daco took them at a rate of knots maybe three or four hundred yards along the road to Blackmill Creek. Then he veered off left where the ground rose, gently at first and then more sharply through a covering of evergreens, which gave off sharp, dry, piny odours. They climbed through the deep forest shade and reached a broad plateau of dense thickets separated by steep-sided gulches. Beyond, the hog-back of Masterman's Ridge stretched grey and black and green into the blue of distance. Here, a general could hide a whole army.

Daco stopped a moment as if he was looking for something. Then he gave a low growl and pointed his mustang into a tangle of bushes, which let them through and closed back behind them. Captain Adams followed Daco into a maze of scattered boulders. No one would find them there.

Daco leaped off his horse, tethered it and scrambled to the top of the tallest rock. From this vantage point, he commanded a wide view of the way they'd come without being seen.

'They've picked up the tracks,' he called down softly. 'They'll be here any time now. I made out four of them.'

He clambered down to join the captain. He took the Winchester from its saddle holster, checked his Colt and took up a position on the left of the trail through the trees they'd come through. Captain Adams did the same on the right.

They did not have long to wait. The drumming of horses, faint at first, grew louder and then stopped.

'Where's the trail go next?' said a voice which Daco recognized as Zeke's.

They heard men dismount and look for tracks.

'Nothing, Zeke,' said another voice. 'It's all loose shale here. Looks like they got away.'

'Luther ain't going to like it,' said Zeke. 'We keep losing men — Lou's got a shot-up knee and now Newt's had his neck broke for him.'

The voices were as clear as if they were at the next table in a barroom. Daco knew that sounds would travel the other way just as easily. It would only take the mustang to snort or the captain's mount to whinny and the game would be up.

'And we need all the hands we got,' went on Zeke. 'There'll be a squad of armed guards waiting for us on the next job. It won't be easy. Come on, mount up. We're doing no good here. Let's get back.'

When they'd gone, the captain took his horse by the reins and walked it through the bushes.

'I'm going after them,' he said. 'I want to know more about this job they talked about.'

'Why take risks? I say we wait and follow them when they leave the house. Meantime, we keep watching them.'

'Maybe you're right at that,' said Captain Adams. 'We've done good work today. There's two less of them than there were this morning. One apiece is a good work rate. I'm with you. We stand down and wait.'

'But not here. We need a place where we got eyes.'

Daco led the way back to Cloudy Bluff and found them an overhang in the valley side hidden by a mass of bushes. From there they had a clear view of the cabin. There was no movement of men, but horses grazed in the paddock.

'Looks like they're still home, Cap'n,' said Daco, reaching for his tobacco sack and offering to roll him a smoke.

The captain shook his head.

'I generally prefer a pipe, Sergeant,' he said and produced a curly briar with a bowl carved with the face of a boxer dog.

'Bonzo,' he said. 'Best darned dog I ever had.'

He lit up and puffed contentedly.

'I been thinking,' said Daco. 'This sergeant and captain stuff's no good. We're still fighting a war but it's not official. Just call me Daco — rhymes with Waco. You got a name I could use for you?'

Captain Adams shifted uncomfortably.

'Sure I got names but I don't use them. Don't like 'em. But sometimes I get called Moose. Because one time I wrestled one. A small one,' he said in an embarrassed afterthought. 'Another time, I was adopted by an Indian tribe. They called me Tondu. They said it means Big Ox. Will that do?'

Daco thought a moment, then grinned. 'Then Tondu it is!'

6

For the next two days, Luther and his boys stayed put in Daco's cabin. From time to time, men ventured out in twos or threes. They scouted round, cautiously at first, and then with growing confidence. Finding no trace of their attackers, they finally assumed the coast was clear.

On the third day, two hours after sunup, the Hayes gang rode out. They took the trail up past Cloudy Bluff and then began travelling at an unhurried lope in the direction of Blackmill Creek. But that was not their destination.

Two miles before they got to town, they forked off south.

'Looks like they're heading for Bridgend,' said Daco. 'Makes sense. It's a big place. It's even got two or three paved streets. A lot more goes on there than Blackmill Creek. Also the railroad goes through it.'

'And maybe it's got a bank or two?' asked Tondu.

'Luther'd be spoilt for choice.'

Daco and Tondu tagged along at a distance behind the group of riders, keeping out of sight. By late afternoon, when Daco reckoned they were a couple of miles from Bridgend, the Hayes gang turned off the road and headed for a deserted farmhouse where it looked like they intended bedding down for the night. There was a well and the men watered their horses. They lit a fire and cooked up bacon and coffee. When all had eaten, two of the group saddled up again, rode back to the road and headed off into town.

One was Luther Hayes, the other Zeke Goodwin.

Daco and Tondu followed.

It was almost dark when the two jayhawkers rode down the main street and hitched their horses to the bar outside the Four Aces Saloon.

Daco and Tondu left their mounts in a side street.

'We need to know why they're here in town. We'll split up,' said Tondu. 'You keep an eye on the front door and I'll get in round the back and see what I can sniff out.'

Daco took up a position in a dark doorway opposite the Four Aces and waited.

Tondu pulled his hat down over his eyes and, taking his time and looking relaxed, strolled across the street. It was early for the saloon crowd but not too late for the good citizens of Bridgend to be still going about their business. He mingled with them before slipping down an alley that ran the length of one side of the saloon. When he reached the back, he made out a flight of wooden stairs leading up to a door on the first floor. With his six-shooter in his fist, he ran lightly up them and paused at the top. The door was unlocked and he stepped inside, closing it behind him.

He found himself in a corridor dimly

lit by candles stuck in sconces on the walls. At the end of it, the light was brighter and he heard the sound of voices and a piano tinkling in the saloon below. He moved quietly past six doors to the six guest rooms and reached the brightly-lit landing. A handrail ran round it and stairs led down from it. Keeping his head well down, he looked through the banisters.

A dozen or so tables were visible. There weren't many customers at this time of day. He saw a man slumped at a table, with his head on his arms, a solitary drinker and a group of tired-looking cowboys concentrating on a poker game. From time to time, one of them would spit a jet of tobacco juice in the general direction of a box of sawdust on the floor that did service as a spittoon. He saw no sign of Luther and Zeke. At the far end of the room a barkeep with a thick moustache and hair parted in the middle was drying glasses with a red cloth and a bored look on his face. Behind the bar was a shelf with a row of bottles on it. There was also a back-bar mirror. In the reflection, Tondu got a view of the space under the landing he was crouching on. He picked out Luther and Zeke at once. They were directly under him, deep in conversation with a lean, angular man dressed entirely in black. His white shirt was held at the neck by a string tie. He wore a smart city suit and matching derby hat. He had bushy eyebrows and a saturnine expression. As far as Tondu could see, he was unarmed.

Tondu straightened up and walked casually down the stairs. No one paid him any heed. He approached the bar and ordered a beer.

Next to him a slurred voice said, 'Buy a man a drink, stranger?'

The voice belonged to an old-timer. His beard was a bird's nest, his eyes were bleary and his shirt and pants were as faded as he was, from being out in all weathers.

Company was the last thing Tondu

wanted. To get rid of him, he said, 'Sure!', produced a couple of dollars and laid them on the bar. The expression on the old-timer's face showed he had made a friend for life. Tondu waved aside his gratitude and as soon as the barkeep served him, he took his drink and wandered unhurriedly with it past the card players and early evening drinkers. He moved to the back of the room, where the landing overhung several tables and sat down unconcernedly with his back to the customers sitting at the next table. Luther, Zeke and the man in the black city suit dropped their voices for a moment, then started up again. Tondu sipped his beer and turned a mildly interested eye over the Four Aces' customers. But all the time, he strained his ears to catch what the three men were saying. They kept their voices low and Tondu had a hard time making sense of the snatches of conversation he managed to pick up.

The words he caught seemed to be

names of places, but they meant nothing to him. One, which sounded like 'Chassen', came up more than the rest. But Luther was obviously getting orders or instructions, for he kept punctuating the low growl of the man in black with 'Sure', and 'Easy' and 'Fine'. Tondu could not get details. In any case, before he could make any sense of what he was half-hearing, the three men got up and left. The moment they were gone, Tondu followed them through the saloon's swinging batwing doors.

Daco was not at his post across the street. Tondu caught sight of him moving carefully along the wooden boardwalk twenty yards behind the three men who had just left the Four Aces. Tondu hurried after him, staying on the opposite sidewalk, and even got a few steps ahead of him, just to let him know he was there.

When the trio reached the end of the street, they turned and walked back the same way, still deep in conversation. This time, as they passed him, Tondu picked up the words 'transfer the goods to the buckboard' before they got out of earshot. When they reached the Four Aces, the man with the string tie and bushy eyebrows paused, said something and went back into the saloon. Luther and Zeke unhitched their horses, mounted up and rode slowly out of town.

Daco and Tondu did not follow. They knew where the two marauders were going: back to join the rest of the gang at the abandoned farmhouse.

'Well, what did you get?' asked Daco.

'Nothing useful. Just a few words. Places, I think. Does 'Chassen' mean anything to you? I think it's a place. But you know the lie of the land better than me.'

'Maybe Chatswen, about five miles east of town,' said Daco. 'Is that all you got?'

'The party in black, who seemed to be giving all the orders and calling the shots, said something about 'transferring the goods to the buckboard'.'

Daco thought a moment.

'So they're planning to steal something that's too heavy for a dozen men to carry in saddle-bags. That's why they need a buckboard.'

'Gold weighs heavy,' said Tondu.

'Right. And what will they transfer it from?'

'A bank vault, maybe? What's this place sounded like Chassen? They got a bank there?' asked Tondu.

'Nope. Chatswen ain't a town.'

'So what is it?'

'A hill,' said Daco. 'The railroad goes that way. I've ridden that train. It's a steep climb and engineers slow a lot as they climb the gradient. By the time they get to the top, a walking man could overtake the loco.'

He thought a moment then said:

'I got it! Every couple of months, it's common knowledge, though no one knows when exactly because the railroad company keeps the details quiet, anyway a train comes in carrying a shipment of gold from the workings around Sacramento and places out West.'

'It fits,' said Tondu excitedly. 'Luther gets tipped off by the man in the black suit who must have a contact on the inside somewhere who lets him in on that little secret. Next day, acting on the information, Luther stops the train on Chatswen Hill and rides off with the shipment. The man in black gets his cut and makes a date for next time. Time a spoke was stuck in their wheels.'

'How d'you reckon we do that?' said Daco.

'I don't like the odds. Twelve against two ain't a winning hand. I say we go to the sheriff and get him to organize a posse. Then we'll stake out the place and take the gang as soon as they show their faces.'

'You're too cautious, Tondu, not to mention complicated. Keep it simple. I trust myself and I trust you but nobody else. Look, if it's extra hands you want, there are bound to be guards on the train. Let's stick to just the two of us linking up with those guards.'

They chewed it this way and that but finally Tondu got his way. He said doing things legal was simplest in the long run. Daco shrugged and went along with it.

'Before we do,' he said, 'let's go take a looksee at our friend in the suit. No reason not to. He don't know us from Adam.'

They walked into the saloon, but the man was not there.

'Maybe he went out the back way,' said Daco, 'or maybe he's renting a room here? Come on, we're wasting time.'

The sheriff's office was at the corner of Main and Adair. A light was burning. When they walked in, a man with a star on his chest was sitting with his boots on his desk, reading a newspaper.

'Howdy, gents,' he said. 'You boys strangers in town?'

Daco quickly explained why they were there. The sheriff put aside his paper and put his feet on the floor, ready for action.

'You sure about this? They're going to rob a train?'

'How else would you figure it?' said Tondu. 'You got the Hayes gang camping on your door-step and a train full of gold passing through tomorrow. You want me to draw a picture?'

'No need to get shirty, son. But I got to do things legal. Judge Prothero needs to be told. I'll go now. You boys won't object to minding the shop while I'm gone?'

Tondu and Daco weren't left long kicking their heels. They heard voices approaching and then footsteps on the boardwalk. The door opened and a lean, angular man in a white shirt, string tie and a black city suit came through the door. There was a gun in his hand.

There was nothing Tondu or Daco could do about it.

'Get their guns, O'Leary,' snapped Judge Prothero. 'These are dangerous men. I know them of old. Lock 'em up! I'll deal with them in the morning!'

7

While Judge Prothero held a gun on the prisoners, Sheriff O'Leary pushed them into a cell and locked them in.

'Where's the others?' barked the judge.

'What others?' said Daco.

'Your associates who also know my business.'

'They're here and there, round and about, ain't that a fact, Daco?' said Tondu carelessly.

The judge paused, looked hard at the prisoners.

'I don't believe you. I think you're on your own. Still,' said the judge turning to Sheriff O'Leary, 'we'd best go take a look and see who else is new in town.'

The two men left.

'Here's a pickle,' said Daco.

''Keep it simple', you said,' replied

Tondu, dropping one eyebrow quizzically and raising the other. 'I'll remember next time. But now, how do we get out of here?'

He immediately began inspecting the cell. The walls were stone and the iron bars of their cage were thick. There was one small high window and a single metal cot with a straw mattress on it. He stood it on its end, climbed up it and looked out of the window.

'Window's barred. Can't even see what's outside. A yard, I think.'

He came down again, righted the cot, sat on it and started to remove his left boot.

Maybe Tondu was a cool dude, Daco thought, the kind of man that can sleep in any circumstances.

'What are you up to? You thinking of turning in?'

'Naw,' said Tondu, who now had the boot in his hand. 'I got a locksmith's patent universal key tucked down the inside here.'

He held up a slender steel rod, with a

flat hook at one end. He put his boot back on and inserted the hook into the lock.

'How long do think we've got before they get back?' he asked while he fished.

'Hard to figure,' said Daco. 'They'll go check out the Four Aces and ask around if anyone's seen new faces and strange men with guns in town. They might even chase a few leads. But it shouldn't take long. So we'd better move fast. How're you doing with that lock?'

'Slow, but I'll get there,' said Tondu, and then he stiffened and stood up.

Footsteps sounded on the boardwalk.

He put the picklock back in his boot and waited.

The door opened and the old-timer with the bird's-nest beard staggered through it, made for the nearest chair and slumped in it. The door swung shut behind him. He was as drunk as a skunk.

'Sheriff! I wanna report a stolen hat,' he said to the empty room. 'That's a hat that's gone and got stole.'

Then it dawned on him there was no one sitting at the desk.

'Where'sh sheriff gone? I wanna report my hat, it's gone. Stole!' he ended with a flourish.

'He just stepped out,' said Tondu.

The old-timer turned his head. His unfocused eyes followed slowly and stopped when they settled on a man in the cell. Two men.

'Say, I know you!' he said in a slurred voice. 'You stood me a drink! You, friend, are the salt of the earth, and if the salt has lost its savour . . .'

He stopped, having lost his thread.

'You can do me a favour in return,' said Tondu. 'We were having a discussion with the sheriff. He reckoned how this is the best jail this side of the Missouri. No one ever got out of this jail once he was locked up in it. We bet him ten dollars it wouldn't hold us. So he locked us in and left us to it, to see if we could get out. Well, if you get those keys from that nail by the door and bring them over here, we'll win the bet for sure and you'll get half the winnings, seeing as how you helped us out.'

'Kenny Cole's the name and I'm your man!' the old-timer exclaimed, getting to his feet. 'One turn deserves another, er, turn.'

Muttering to himself, he headed for the keys, unhooked them and brought them unsteadily to Tondu who was holding out a five dollar bill. Kenny stopped just short of him.

'Is that for me?'

'Sure is, when you hand over those keys.'

'I ain't had one of those green beauties in my hand since the day . . . I don't know when.'

He took one step forward, then stopped again.

'I came by to report a missing hat. Saturday nights I gen'ally come and report my hat got stole. Sheriff just locks me up for the night, 'specially when it's raining or cold. Him and me go back a long way. I mind me one time — '

To stop him wandering off down

memory lane, Tondu broke in.

'And this here's my partner, Taters O'Hara. They call me Jawbone Jones. Come and say hello to Taters.'

Kenny looked up. The keys rattled in his hand. He started walking again and kept coming.

'Sure glad to meet you, Kenny,' said Taters O'Hara, drawing him on.

'Likewise I'm sure.'

Tondu put one arm through the bars and took the keys from Kenny's outstretched hand. Working through the bars, he selected one from the bunch, reversed it, inserted it in the lock and turned. There was a click and the door opened when he pushed it.

Kenny immediately stepped inside like a weary traveller reaching home after a long, long journey. He made straight for the iron cot, lay down on it and immediately went to sleep. Tondu hesitated a moment, then tucked the five-dollar bill into his waistcoat pocket.

'Nice doing business with you, Kenny.'

He locked the cell door behind them. While Daco retrieved their gun-belts from the chair where O'Leary had dumped them, Tondu put the keys back on their nail.

'Give the sheriff something to think about, figuring how we got out and away,' he winked.

They hurried up the dark street. They had to get out of town fast, before they ran into Judge Prothero.

It was late and there were few people about. The windows of the Four Aces were still lit but the place was almost as peaceful as a spinster's parlour. Tondu took a peek through a window: no one there who looked like trouble. He and Daco walked on. The horses were still where they had left them. They mounted and rode out of town on the road to Blackmill Creek.

When they'd left the last buildings behind them, Daco said:

'Luther's smarter than I gave him credit for. How in tarnation did he manage to get a judge and a sheriff in his pocket? It means he can go round doing pretty much as he likes and know he'll never get done for it.'

'Money, old friend,' said Tondu. 'Most people have got a price.'

Daco chewed on this then put the matter out of his mind. There were more urgent things to think about.

'What have we got to go on?' he asked. 'A town with banks and a gang of jayhawkers camped just outside waiting to rob it, or a gang bedded down five miles from a gradient where a train carrying gold is due to pass any day. How will Luther jump? The bank won't have armed guards defending it, but the train offers richer pickings.'

'He'll go for the train. Luther never ducked a fight in his life — he enjoys a scrap. But the clincher is the judge. He won't want him making trouble robbing a bank on his doorstep. Too close to home.'

'That's the way I see it too, so let's go stake out Chatswen Hill,' said Daco.

'But first, we'll take a look at

Luther's camp. See if anything's stirring there.'

The moon was not yet up, but the sky was strewn with stars. Tondu and Daco approached the abandoned farm with caution. They picked out a lone sentry by the red glow of his cigarette. Apart from him and the occasional horse snickering in its dreams, there was no other hint of life. The Hayes gang were hunkered down for the night. Daco and Tondu left them to their slumber.

Soon the moon was up and it made the going easy. It took the two men something over an hour to reach Chatswen Hill. They climbed the slope and looked down the length of the track. The twin moon-silvered snakes of the rails took the eye far away into the distance.

'By the time the loco gets this far, it'll be going no faster than a man walking,' said Daco. 'Now if you were going to jump the train, where would you do it from?'

They looked the terrain over, discussed the options and finally hit on a stand of pines which would give just the right cover for a gang of *bandidos*. It was no more than thirty yards from the track. The attackers could wait until the last moment before showing their hand. It would all be over before the guards knew what was happening.

They chose a position on the opposite side of the tracks to the pines. There they would have an unimpeded view of the pines and clear lines of fire. They unsaddled the horses and tethered them in a hollow in a clump of cottonwoods. Daco rustled up some coffee which they drank as they ate some biscuits and cold bacon. Tondu slept for a couple of hours until Daco woke him and he in turn got some shut-eye while his partner kept watch.

Daco was shaken out of his sleep by Tondu. The sun was already up.

'Take a look,' said Tondu.

He peered carefully through the bushes at the pines on the other side of the tracks. It looked peaceful enough, but then he saw a metallic glint among the leaves. Could have been the rowel of a spur. But it was just as likely to be the barrel of a gun.

'I was starting to think today wasn't the day the train comes through or that there'd been a change of plan,' said Tondu. 'Then I saw Luther's gang coming up the hill. They headed straight for the pines. They're there now. Any idea when the train's due?'

'Listen, Tondu, I just thought of something. We're here waiting for them boys to come out of the trees. Then we pick 'em off, right?'

'Right.'

'Can your gun shoot through solid trains? If it can't you're not going to shoot anybody. We're in the wrong place! We should be to their rear, not facing them! Picture it. The loco comes along puffing like a grampus. Luther and his boys ride out to stop it. How are we supposed to shoot 'em dead with a train between us and them?'

8

The moment before, they'd had all the time in the world. No need to make a move till they saw the smoke from the loco's chimney way down on the plain. They'd have plenty of warning.

But now they saddled up in a rush. To hold on to the advantage of surprise, they were going to have to cross the tracks somehow and get behind the Hayes gang. It wouldn't be easy. If they were spotted, they'd be sitting ducks. They took off hell for leather down the slope, keeping parallel to the tracks, looking for a place lower down where they could cross unseen.

They were half way down when they saw smoke.

Too late! There was no way now of carrying out their plan. They reined in and stopped.

'Only one thing we can do now. We

got to warn the guards on the train,' said Tondu.

'And how are we going to do that?' said Daco.

But Tondu had touched his horse's side with his boot heels and was away. Daco's mustang, sensing the urgency of the moment, took off fast after him.

They galloped down the slope for another half mile towards the train which was now coming towards them and picking up speed to take the gradient ahead. When it was still a couple of hundred yards off, Daco stopped, jumped down, stood plumb in the middle of the tracks and waved his hat to attract attention. Tondu rode on.

The engineer saw him and sounded his warning signal but didn't slow down. That was company policy. Engineers had orders not to stop anywhere outside regular stations unless there was a good reason to. It was always possible a man might have a very good reason for trying to stop a train, track up ahead washed away by storms or blocked by a herd crossing the rails. Could be this man waving his hat was trying to warn him of a hazard up ahead. The engineer hesitated. The man held his ground. The engineer slowed . . .

Meanwhile, when Tondu got to within fifty yards of the train, he turned his mount and rode back the way he'd come, the train gained on him, caught up and started passing. He waved his hat to attract attention, but the loco went on drawing away. It was almost past him when it started to slow, though whether this was because he'd been spotted or for some other reason he couldn't tell. But now he found himself keeping pace with the rear cars. The last one had an observation platform. On it, a man was leaning on the rail, smoking a cigarette. He was slim built and lean and wore a marshal's badge pinned to his chest. When he saw Tondu galloping by the side of the train, he reached for his gun. Then he gave a start, holstered his weapon, held out one hand and pulled him on to the platform.

Daco had been keeping an eye on Tondu's progress down the side of the train. When he saw him being pulled on board, he knew the guards would be tipped off. But he didn't think they'd want the train to stop. They'd want it to go on its way, so they could take on the ambushers. He stepped off the track, put his hat back on his head and as the loco passed him he shouted to the engineer to pick up speed again. He waited until the last car was almost on him, spurred his horse forward until it was level with him and swung himself up on to the platform. A guard pointed a gun at him. Daco raised his arms and then dropped them again when a voice barked an order for the guard to put his gun up. He turned and saw Tondu and, standing next to him, a man with a badge. There was a kind of loose-limbed insolence about him, which was offset by a ready, friendly grin. A cigarette was screwed into the corner of his mouth.

'Daco, meet my good friend Marshal Barrington Davies. We were in the War and after it was over we chased jayhawkers together.'

'Just call me Barrie, we'll talk later,' the marshal said. 'But I'm glad to hear you're gunning for Luther Hayes too.'

The loco had picked up speed again as it needed to if it was to make the gradient. But it began to slow as the slope started to take its toll. Leaving Tondu and Daco on the platform of the observation car, Barrie went inside and gave last-minute orders. In the light of the information Tondu had brought him, he concentrated his sharp-shooters on the right-hand side of the train where the main attack would come from when the pace had slowed right down. A half-dozen men were posted at the car windows. The rest, about twenty in all, stood ready and waiting for the signal to jump off the train, spread out and attack the ambushers from the side and rear.

Daco looked out the window. Up ahead was the stand of pines. Nothing moved. He had a sudden thought:

perhaps Luther had heard them ride off or maybe had seen him in the middle of the track waving his hat, and had cleared out. He was not a church-going man but he sent up a little prayer that Luther and his boys had stayed put. Every slow turn of the train's wheels was bringing him nearer to the moment when he would face the man who had murdered his Ginny . . .

The train had now slowed to a fast walk. The clump of pines was no more than fifty yards ahead. Still no sign of life.

'C'mon, c'mon!' he muttered.

Then there was a commotion in the trees and the first of a dozen riders burst into the clear and began making straight towards the train, yelling and loosing off shots at the loco's footplate. Their first task was to stop it and the best way of doing that was to snuff out the engineer and his crew.

The sharp-shooters on the train returned their fire. At first, they had clear targets and Daco saw two of

Hayes' men go down. But the angle soon narrowed until there was nothing for them to shoot at. They put up their guns and followed the rest of the squad who had left the train and fanned out, firing as they went. Suddenly, the train came to a sudden stop and the lurch sent Daco and Tondu sprawling.

It felt as if the emergency brake had been applied. The engineer had probably stopped a bullet.

'C'mon, let's join the party,' said Tondu.

They jumped down and ran half the length of the train on the blind side of the battle, looking for a gap between cars to shoot through. Barrie had said the gold was in the fourth car from the front. Luther, tipped off by Judge Prothero, would know it too and would make straight for it. They were half way along when one of his men snuck under the rods and stood up. He'd had enough and had decided to make a getaway. Tondu called for him to stop. His answer was to reach for his six-gun but he was too slow. Before he could pull the trigger, he staggered, made a grab for the side of the train, then fell in a heap. There was a neat hole in the front of his shirt. Tondu put up his smoking gun.

All of a sudden, there was an explosion, which came from a car no more than fifteen yards ahead of them.

'It's the payload car,' cried Daco. 'Luther's blown his way in.'

There was a short lull and then the shooting began again with redoubled fury. Luther's men had taken up positions inside the car. They were pinned down but were clearly in no mood to give up. Luther was heard ordering them to shoot only when they had a target, to save ammo. Meanwhile, there were sounds of what could have been metal boxes being yanked open with crowbars.

Then the shooting stopped and a voice cried:

'Hayes! This is US Marshal Davies. You remember me, Luther?'

'Maybe I do,' came the reply. 'What d'you want?'

'Throw your weapons down and come out of there with your hands up!'

'I ain't finished what I'm doing, Marshal, and I always finish what I start!'

There was a salvo of shots from the car. At almost the same time, Daco and Tondu saw the side of the car with the gold bulge and then split as the planks were shattered by a small charge. The blast was unexpected and, not being prepared for it, they were left momentarily dazed. Then the dust and smoke cleared, and they saw a hole in the side of the car. Twenty yards to their left, half a dozen men were running towards the cover where Tondu and Daco had spent the previous night. Tondu's gun had been blown out of his hand, but Daco managed to get off a few shots. However, he was still dizzy from the explosion and his bullets went wide.

Then Barrie's men poured through the car and set off on foot in hot pursuit. Tondu and Daco, still groggy, started shooting at the fleeing men. Two went down, then a third. There were more shots and then the sound of gunfire stopped. The marshal returned with his men.

'They got away,' he said. 'Three of 'em. Used your horses, boys. Ain't that something?'

'Well, I'll be damned!' said Daco. 'Those nags must have followed the train up the slope!'

'And gone back to the place where we tethered them last night,' said Tondu. 'Must have remembered the grass was sweet.'

'Can't be helped,' said the marshal, drawing on the cigarette that never seemed to leave his lips. 'That apart, it's been a good day's work. Luther got away on one horse and two others doubled on the mustang. But his gang's finished. All dead or wounded. On our side we took one killed and two wounded.'

He paused and turned to one of his men:

'Go check on the damage to that bullion car. I want to know if it's in a fit state to roll.'

He took out the makings and lit another smoke.

'Luther won't have had time to grab much loot, if any,' he went on. 'So I won't be going after him. If the bullion car isn't fit to roll, we'll have to uncouple her and tip her off the track. That'll take time. But if she can stay on them bogeys, we'll be on our way within the hour. Won't even make a small dent in the schedule. Want to tag along with us?'

'I can't speak for Tondu,' said Daco, 'but I ain't going to let Luther's trail go cold. If I lose him now, God knows when I'd find him again. It's not his robbing ways I care about; I want him for myself.'

'Fair enough,' said Barrie. 'What do you say, Tondu? If you boys are intending to stay hereabouts, you can spread the word about what's happened here. People would be more prepared to listen to a man with a star. You were a marshal once and there's no reason why you shouldn't be again. I could swear you in temporary here and now. Make it regular later.'

'Thanks Barrie, but I think I'll stick with Daco for now. My life's got more interesting since we joined up.'

'Don't be hasty, Tondu,' said Daco. 'Think. Judge Prothero and the sheriff have got dirty hands. But only we know and they are the law hereabouts. They'd just put us behind bars the moment we showed our faces in town. But if you had a star on your shirt front, you could make life harder for them.'

'Daco's right,' said Barrie. 'You can have my badge. I don't need it. My men know who I am.'

Tondu thought a moment then saw the sense of what Daco had said. A few moments later, after he'd said the necessary words about promising to uphold the law and serve justice, Barrie pinned a star on his chest.

'And now,' he asked, 'what exactly are you proposing to do?'

'I reckon Luther will head back to Bridgend,' said Tondu. 'He'll want to have words with Judge Prothero.'

'Do you think the Railroad Company will be offering a reward?' asked Daco.

'They often do,' said Barrie, frowning with disapproval. Tondu's new friend sounded too mercenary for his taste.

'I don't mean cash. But if you could spare a couple of horses, we'd be mighty grateful. Luther's got a head start and we ain't going to catch him up on foot.'

Barrie's face lightened. 'Sure. We got horses in the guard's car. We always carry a few on jobs like this in case we need to mount a pursuit. But like I said, I ain't going after them boys. I got to stay with the train. Can't afford the delay. But you're welcome to take your pick.'

A half hour later, Daco was sitting on a feisty roan and Tondu had a grey to ride.

'Wish I was coming with you,' said Barrie. 'But I got a job to do. I intend to see this train gets through.'

The damaged bullion car was fit to roll and the gold had been transferred to another, which was duly locked and sealed. The fireman, deputizing for the engineer who'd been shot, released the brake and started the train moving. The wheels spun until they found enough traction to shift the load it was hauling and slowly the train began to inch forward.

Barrie, standing on the footplate, shouted, 'Good hunting! See you around!'

Daco and Tondu waved and then put spur to flank.

9

Luther Hayes's face was black with fury. Someone had welshed on him! Otherwise, how would a trap have been laid for him to walk into? The marshal must have had over twenty men on that train. He'd been out-thought and out-gunned. With most of his men killed or taken, he was lucky to have got out in one piece. And he wasn't clear yet. At his back, he could hear the marshal's men crashing through the brush.

Out of the corner of his eye he saw Zeke and the new man, what was his name, Kelly, John Kelly. So, just three of them had got away. But then he knew Lady Luck hadn't given up on him. There, in the trees, two horses were grazing, one a good-looking mustang, the other a big black stallion, all saddled up and ready to go. He grinned. He motioned to Zeke and Kelly who'd also spotted their ticket to freedom.

They slowed down so as not to frighten the nags, which looked up at them with interest. Luther grabbed the reins of the mustang and swung up into the saddle. Zeke climbed onto the black stallion and at a word from Luther, pulled Kelly up behind him. Luther had already taken off fast. Zeke urged his mount after him.

A few shots zinged around them and then stopped. They were out of range. Luther slowed to a quick canter and looked back to check there was no one coming after them. No one was, which told him that the marshal's guards didn't have anything to ride. He stopped and waited for Zeke to catch him up.

'Where to, Luther?' he asked.

'We're going to see the judge. We was sold down the river, Zeke, and I aim to find out the who and the how and the why of it.'

'I'm all for it, Luther. But we can't just go bustin' in on Judge Prothero.

He's an important man. We'd stir up a hornet's nest.'

'Hell, I been stirring up them things since I was a kid in galluses and knee britches.'

But Zeke had the last word. They hung back, waiting for the sun to dip under the horizon before riding into town. Until dusk came, they stopped in the shade of a stand of whispering cottonwood trees and smoked.

'What sort of haul we get, Zeke?'

While Luther had been holding off the guards, Zeke had crow-barred a number of metal boxes. He'd grabbed what he could, put it in a pouch and slung it round his neck. Now he removed it and passed it to Luther.

'See for yourself,' he said.

'It don't weigh heavy,' said Luther.

'Paper money. It was the best I could do. Ingots is too big to fit in a man's pants' pocket. Anyhow, there were men with guns shooting at us at the time,' he added wryly.

Luther grunted. He weighed the

pouch in his hand, lifting it up and down to get the feel of it. Then he teased the drawstring open and peered inside.

'No more'n five hundred dollars here,' he said in disgust.

'That ain't much of a payday,' said John Kelly. 'Maybe we can squeeze a mite more out of the judge. He'll be good for a couple of thousand at least.'

'Too damn right,' said Luther. 'Let's go lean on him.'

'What about that other business, Luther?' asked Zeke. 'Have you given up on that rat Ward who got us sent down?'

'I ain't forgot the skunk,' said Luther. 'He's still top of the list. But the train job was too good to pass up on. First we go see the judge and get us some dollars. Then we go back to Ward's place and settle his hash. He'll turn up sooner or later. That way we kill two birds with one stone. We get him and somewhere to hide up until the fuss has died down.'

Suddenly all three men froze at the rattle of an approaching cart. They were well enough hidden, but they had no wish to draw attention to themselves. They peered through the gathering gloom and saw a flatboard rig, a driver and two men in back. As it passed, not more than thirty yards away, Kelly stood up and moved out of the cottonwoods.

'It's all right, Luther,' he said. 'It's only Clip and a couple of the boys.'

Clip Curtz explained how he, Duffy and Rees had retreated back into the pines, laid low and waited for things to go quiet and it was safe to make a move. They'd lost their horses, which had been panicked when the shooting started, but the rig they'd brought to carry the gold was still where it had been tethered. They'd headed off along the trail back to Bridgend where they thought Luther would make for too.

'You saw the train move off, Clip. Were the marshal and all his men on it?'

'They sure were. They checked out

the bullion car and moved the gold into another. Then they went on their way. They'll be miles away now. No chance of catching them if that's what you're thinking.'

'Did they all get on the train?' said Zeke.

'They left two behind.'

'Why?' snapped Luther.

'How should I know? So they'd have somebody to wave them goodbye, mebbe.'

Luther hit Clip in the mouth, not hard enough to knock him down but hard enough to make him buckle at the knees.

'I asked you why the marshal left a couple of men by the side of the track!'

While Clip wiped the blood off his split lip, Zeke asked:

'What did the two men look like? Did you recognize them?'

Clip said none of them had ever seen them before.

'But one was riding a roan,' said Duffy.

'And the other a grey stallion,' said Rees.

'Know what, Luther?' said Zeke. 'My money says those two fellers were Ward and his sidekick.'

Luther thought for a moment.

'This gets better and better. We've got three extra guns on side, the marshal ain't coming after us and all we got to do is wait for Ward to come to us.'

'And meantime we're damn near broke,' said Zeke. 'Time we went to see the judge.'

They went back to the farm. Clip and the other two gunslingers, Duffy and Rees, stayed there with the rig, while Luther, Zeke and Kelly rode into Bridgend. No one gave then a second glance. Three is friends; six is a raiding party.

News of the train hold-up had yet to reach the town where it was business as usual. The three men walked their horses down the main street, passed the Four Aces and made straight for Judge Prothero's house. His housekeeper opened the door, looked at them suspiciously but showed them into the judge's study.

'Didn't I tell you never to come here?' snarled the judge the moment the door was shut. 'I can't afford to be seen associating with you. I told you plain.'

'Don't you want to know how the job went?' asked Luther. 'Since you haven't asked, I'll tell you. We walked into a trap. I lost most of my boys, killed or captured, and only just managed to get away myself. It was a set-up and you're going to come clean.'

Next moment, Luther was pointing a big gun in the judge's face.

'Don't be a fool, Hayes. Put that away. Why would I set you up? I had no reason to want the job to go wrong. I arranged it because I needed the money.'

Luther considered this for a moment. He glanced across at Zeke who gave a brief nod.

Luther lowered his gun.

'If things are like you say, how come the marshal knew the exact spot where we were going to hit the train?'

'Luther, I just remembered,' said John Kelly. 'Clean forgot. While we was waiting for the loco to come up the gradient and getting ready for it, Clip pointed to a man on the track, mebbe half a mile or more down the slope. He was either being attacked by a swarm of bees or trying to attract the driver's eye. Clip said he thought he'd seen another man down there, too, but he couldn't rightly say what they were up to. And then we were attacked and all hell broke loose.'

'Maybe that explains the horses we found,' said Zeke.

'Two men?' said the judge. 'What did they look like?'

'Clip didn't say. Anyways, they were too far off.'

'Why do you want to know?' asked Luther.

'Because two men turned up last night at the sheriff's office. Said they knew the train was going to be ambushed on Chatswen Hill. The sheriff fetched me and we locked them up in the cells. I thought they might not be alone so we went out to check. When we got back to question them and find out how they knew about the hold-up, they'd gone.'

It was Luther's turn to ask: 'What did they look like?'

'One was real big. Dark hair, carried himself well. The other was about the same age, thirty-five or forty, a bit taller than Zeke. The big man called him by his name. Damned if I can remember. Unusual name. I got it! Daco! That's it.'

'Get O'Leary here,' snapped Luther.

But the sheriff wasn't able to provide any more information, though he'd worked out how the prisoners had managed their escape. Kenny Coles had felt his boot in the seat of his pants.

'So now they know the judge is mixed up in all this,' said Zeke. 'It's the only lead they've got, so they'll be back. When they show up, we'll be waiting. We'll make them cough up everything.'

'Very well,' said the judge. 'I'll leave it to you. But keep me out of it. You must also let me know exactly what's going on. I can't help you if I don't know what's happening. Now, how much did you get away with?'

Zeke tossed the pouch onto the judge's desk.

The judge peeked inside, then without even bothering to count the contents, he looked up furiously.

'It comes to five hundred,' said Zeke icily.

'Is that all? It's nowhere near enough. It means starting again. No matter, I'll find another job you can pull. It won't pay as well but it'll have to do. I already have half an idea.'

He thought a moment.

'Here's what we do.'

But before he could explain, Luther leaned across the desk and scooped the leather bag out of his hands.

'A lot of my boys went down for this. I reckon we got a right to it.'

'And to as much and more again,' said Zeke. 'We took a lot of risks to get it, mister, and we deserve to be paid.'

For a moment, the judge looked as if he was going to argue. He had a gun in his drawer and he was handy with it. In his time he'd made a lot of enemies. He'd learned how to look after himself. Then his face relaxed and he smiled.

'You're right, I have been remiss. I should have thought of it myself. Here, take the five hundred,' he said, rising to his feet. 'I can't match it right now — I don't keep that sort of money in the house — but give me a moment, and I'll see what I can raise.'

He crossed to a door, which he opened with two keys. He went inside and was about to lock it behind him, as he always did, when Luther pushed him in and followed. The room was lined with shelves. On the shelves were Prothero's law-books and, in a corner, a small safe.

'Open it,' said Luther.

The judge sighed, tripped the combination, pulled the door open and stepped back. Luther reached in and pulled out a small wad of bills.

'This all there is?' he snarled.

'I told you, Hayes. You should listen more. I'm strapped just now. That's why I set up the train job. At the moment, you've got more cash than I have.'

Luther pushed him back into his study and tossed the wad to Zeke. Zeke counted it.

'Six hundred,' he said.

Luther held out his hand for the money and slipped it into his back pants pocket.

'This'll do for now,' he said.

'Oh, very well,' said the judge. 'But there's plenty more where that came from, if we play our cards right. Are you boys ready for another foray?'

Luther nodded.

'But you must do exactly what I say. I'm going to need a day or two to set it up. Meantime, I want you to disappear. Find a place and hole up in it. Round up a few more men — three or four will be enough. Leave this man here. What's your name?'

'Kelly, Your Honour, John Kelly.'

'Leave John in town with me. He can get a room at the Four Aces. But make sure he keeps his mouth shut. I don't want our business spread all over town. When I'm ready, I'll send him to let you know what you're to do. Got that?'

Luther thought a moment and then got another nod from Zeke.

'I'll give you a second chance, Judge. But this time, if anything goes wrong, I'll kill you.'

Judge Prothero smiled a thin smile.

'No you won't, Luther. You're not that much of a fool that you don't know it's never a good idea to shoot a judge. Judges have always got friends in high places. They stick together. They've got an interest in watching their own backs. They'd see to it that you were hunted down and when they caught you they'd hang you. A painful way of leaving this wicked world. Still, I understand why your feelings are running high. I'm grateful to you for being frank. Now we both know where we stand.'

'Maybe,' said Zeke, who hadn't said

much. 'But we still don't know how Ward and his friend knew we were going to hit a gold train on Chatswen Hill on the day and time we did. We wouldn't want that sort of thing to happen again. Bad for business.'

Judge Prothero scowled.

'Leave it to me. I'll get to the bottom of it,' he said.

10

Daco didn't bother to knock. He opened the door to the sheriff's office with his right boot.

O'Leary was on his feet in an instant and reaching for his gun.

'Go on, act like it's my birthday,' Tondu said pleasantly, pointing his shooter at the sheriff.

Daco picked up the gun-belt the sheriff had dropped at Tondu's command and tossed it into a corner.

'Time to talk, Sheriff. What have you and the judge been getting into?'

'I don't know what you're talking about,' O'Leary spluttered, as he recovered from the shock. 'Anyhow, you can't come barging in here. I'm the law in this town and what you're doing could end up with the two of you dangling at the end of a rope.'

Tondu pulled up a chair and sat down.

'I don't think it'll come to that. If

there's any hanging business needs looking after,' he said, 'I'm the one who'll be attending to it.'

And so saying, he flipped back the lapel of his vest.

'You're a US marshal?' said O'Leary in disbelief.

'Sure am. And this here's my deputy,' he said, with a nod in Daco's direction.

'What brings you to Bridgend?' said O'Leary suspiciously. 'This is a quiet town. It minds its own business. Nothing going on here that warrants a visit from any snooping marshal.'

'Not everybody would agree that it's as law-abiding a place as you say, Sheriff. Information is laid before you that a train is going to be robbed. What do you do? You bring in a judge who locks up the informants without asking questions. Is that how you administer justice hereabouts?'

'I can explain . . . ' began O'Leary. But he didn't get any further. He put his head in his hands, the picture of despair.

'You're right, Marshal,' he said, looking

up, suddenly angry. 'But the place and the folks ain't rotten. Just Judge Prothero.'

'If you're so clean, how come you locked us up like you were the judge's pet dog fetching a stick for him?'

'It's complicated. You wouldn't understand.'

'Try me,' said acting marshal Tondu Adams.

O'Leary looked up, hesitated a moment then decided he had no choice. Straightening up, he began:

'I been in jail. Back in Denver. It happened a dozen years ago. Did time for robbing a stage, though I swear to God I was innocent. There'd been a lot of hold-ups and the mayor, the local gazette and most of the town folk were calling for action to put an end to it. The court needed a conviction, a culprit. I happened to walk by and they grabbed me because I couldn't prove I was someplace else when the stick-up took place. Oh they knew I had nothing to do with any of it, but they wanted a fall guy. The court handed down a five year stretch. It was a stitch-up. The judge and all the lawyers were in on it, but I don't think they all liked it. Nor did they relish the idea of me hanging around in the state pen where I might make trouble. Anyways, that's what my defence attorney told me. It was he who arranged for me to climb over the jail wall a couple of months later. His name was Prothero.

'When I got out, I drifted around and years later finished up here. The first man I saw when I arrived was lawyer Prothero. But now he was this important judge. His word was law. He gave me a job running errands, escorting him around and such like. When the sheriff's position came up for annual re-election, he put my name forward, saying how I was an experienced man, and trustworthy. With him speaking up for me, I was shoe-horned into the job. At the time I thought he'd done it because he owed me for getting me jailed back in Denver. But I soon found out that what he wanted was a badge hanging on the shirt of a man who'd do what he was told, jail his opponents and run his enemies out of town. That way, whatever he did had the backing of the law. If I jibbed, he threatened to inform on me, let it be known I was an escaped felon and get me sent back to the penitentiary. He had me over a barrel. Ever since, I been fielding all the sticks he throws. And know what?'

He paused.

'I'm tired of it. Here, take this.'

He unpinned his badge and handed it to Tondu who took it, thought for a moment and then gave it back.

'I didn't appoint you, so I'm not in a position to accept your resignation.'

He paused, his clear grey eyes fixed on the sheriff's face. He glanced up at Daco who hesitated then nodded.

'I heard you out, Sheriff, and liked what I heard. So did my colleague. I think you're ready to turn over a new leaf, as they say. I'm ready to give you a second chance.'

'New leaves mostly don't stay turned

for long,' said Daco. 'But I've seen it happen. Before I chip in with my final ten cents' worth, I want you to put us in the picture about your friend the judge. Fair enough?'

Now that O'Leary had got his secret off his chest, he was only too eager to prove that he was not the judge's bagman.

He said he knew exactly what Judge Prothero was up to. Since Bridgend had got the railroad, its population had grown fast and the land roundabout had been snapped up by homesteaders and small ranchers. The last of the Ogwy Indians had gone to reservations and Ogmore County had prospered, thanks mainly to cattle. But cattle needed grass and grass needed water. The fact was that there wasn't enough rain to support the demand for all the water that was needed. The flatlands had been overgrazed, and even Peace Valley, which was higher and not so badly affected, was turning into a dustbowl. Homesteaders and smaller ranchers who had settled there were selling up and moving on. But there were state plans to build a dam which would supply enough water to re-establish lush pasture for a sustainable level of cattle raising. Architect-made plans had been accepted and soon company bids would be compared and vetted and contracts handed out.

From the time the project was mooted, Judge Prothero had been making his own plans. He wasn't interested in bidding for building contracts. Instead, he'd set up a company to buy out the homesteaders at a time when their land was worthless. Properties he bought up cheap would fetch high prices from the day the successful bidding company started acquiring land in Peace Valley, which would have to be flooded to catch the spring rains that poured down from the high mountains.

'The upshot is,' concluded O'Leary, 'that as of now Judge Prothero owns a big slice of Peace Valley. He bought out owners who were only too grateful for the pittance he offered them. If any refused he sent thugs out to lean on them and make them see that refusing his offer wasn't good for their health. In the end, they all took what he offered. The way they saw it, they wouldn't get a better deal. Anyway, what choice did they have?'

'If he already owns most of Peace Valley, why does he need money bad enough to use the likes of Luther Hayes to rob trains for him? When is enough enough? How much money does he want?'

'More,' said O'Leary simply. 'Always more.'

'So when the construction company that wins the contract comes along and starts acquiring land to flood, the judge will sell it to them at many times the price he paid for it,' said Tondu.

Daco whistled.

'He'll clean up! What'll he do then. Retire?'

'He don't confide in me,' said O'Leary. 'But he's not the sort who inclines to girls and cards and high living. I reckon he'll go in for politics, buy himself a governorship somewhere.'

'You're right,' said Tondu. 'He sounds like a man who enjoys power above any other dad-blamed thing.'

'Since you boys put paid to the plan he cooked up to rob the train out on Chatswen Hill, I got some news you'll find mighty pleasing.'

And he told how he'd been summoned to the judge's house to tell what he knew about the men who'd got out of his jail. Luther was there with two others and he was complaining that he had lost half his men.

'Those odds are coming down all the time,' grinned Daco.

'The judge said he was working on another plan. Luther's gang were to be part of it, but it wasn't ready so I can't tell you more except that Luther was to make himself scarce for a few days. They arranged for one of the gang, John Kelly is his name, to hang out in the Four Aces until the judge sends him to fetch Luther back.'

'Any idea what job is he planning?' asked Tondu.

'Nope,' said O'Leary, 'but I don't think we need to look far. Day after tomorrow there's a big cattle fair starts in Newbridge Fields, down by the river. There's maybe four, five herds due in for shipping by rail back East. There'll be a lot of beef sold and bought, a lot of money changing hands and a lot of money going into banks. Chances are the judge will have an eye to it. I reckon he's going to rob a bank. Probably Dawson's Bank. It's the one the cattlemen use most.'

'Give the man his badge back, Tondu,' said Daco with a grin. 'I reckon he's serious about that new leaf.'

'Thanks, boys,' said O'Leary. 'I sure appreciate it. I want to see Judge Prothero stopped as much as you want to stop Luther in his tracks.'

'Good,' said Tondu. 'But we ain't finished yet. You said Luther left a man in the Four Aces. What say we mosey along and see what he's got to say for himself?'

The Four Aces was lit up like a birthday cake. Raucous voices sang along to the same out-of-tune piano but were at times drowned out by a rising and ebbing tide of shouting, arguing and angry words, for on pay nights genial high spirits quickly turned mean and fuses were short.

Tondu and Daco decided it was best if they didn't show their faces, so O'Leary went in. Once through the swing doors, he was hit by a wall of sound. The place was full of noise, men and smoke and it took him a couple of minutes to locate Kelly, who was sitting at a table under the landing at the back of the room. O'Leary managed to grab himself a beer. He took it across to where Kelly was concentrating on a hand of cards, which he seemed to like fine, for he turned down the offer of another two. O'Leary drank his beer. Then he said:

'John, he wants you.'

'Not now,' said Kelly. 'Can't you see I'm playing cards here?'

'You want me to say you're too busy to come?'

Kelly looked up, his face twisted with anger. Then he threw his cards down, stood up and barged his way to the door. The cowboys he jostled yelled at him and he snarled back. O'Leary followed.

When they were outside, Kelly swore and said:

'Three kings and a pair of tens, dammit! And he chooses that moment to pull me out of the hottest seat I had in a long time. What's he want?'

'You'll have to ask him.'

They walked on. Behind them, two figures followed, keeping to the shadows.

'This ain't the way to his house,' said Kelly suspiciously.

'Sure ain't,' agreed O'Leary. 'We ain't going to his house. The judge is in my office.'

'What's he doing there?'

'Ain't no good asking me. I'm just the dog that fetches the sticks.'

'That's about the size of it too,' Kelly leered. 'It sure ain't work for a man.'

O'Leary took it without reacting.

And then they were at his office. The sheriff opened the door and Kelly walked in and before he knew what was happening, two other men had followed him inside. They had guns in their hands. The guns were pointing at him.

'Drop your belt on the ground,' said Daco. 'Nice and slow.'

Kelly did what he was told. O'Leary picked up his gun-belt, stowed it away in a cupboard, and then sat him down on a chair and tied his hands behind him.

'What's this all about, O'Leary?' he growled.

'I retired from fetching sticks, John,' said the sheriff. 'You were right. It's not a job for a man.'

'Who are these two?' asked Kelly, transferring his attention to Tondu and Daco.

'Old pals of Luther Hayes,' said Tondu. 'We go back a long way. Where's he at right now?'

'I don't know who you're talking about.'

'Watch your lip when you talk to a US marshal,' said Daco pleasantly. 'Tondu, show him your star.'

Tondu obliged. Kelly gulped.

'Anyways, we know where he's at,' said Tondu. 'He's hiding out at that abandoned farm outside town, close by the Blackmill Creek cut-off.'

'I don't know no Luther Hayes. I'm just passing through.'

'Sheriff here says different. You calling him a liar?'

Kelly swallowed again.

'You are what the lawyers call a 'known associate' of a wanted man. That means,' said Tondu, happily making it up as he went along, 'that you'll get sent down for a long stretch when your case comes up in court.'

Kelly brightened: 'Not if Judge Prothero has any say in it.'

'He won't,' said Tondu. 'He's a known associate of Luther Hayes too. They'll lock him up and throw the key away. You could end up sharing a cell with him. You'll have a lot to talk about.'

Kelly swallowed hard. He didn't like the sound of it. He'd been in jail before, more than once. He preferred life on the outside.

'Still, nobody's interested in the dog that fetches the sticks, John,' said O'Leary. 'The marshal here ain't concerned with you, only with what you know. Luther's the man he's after. Now, if you could see your way clear to giving helpful answers to certain questions, I dare say it would be taken into account.'

'Sheriff's right,' said Tondu. 'Courts always like a stoolie.'

The word hit Kelly like the lash of a whip. For all that, it looked like his best, his only way out of the fix he was in.

'All right,' he growled. 'What can I tell you?'

'Start after you got back to town after

121

raiding the train.'

'You know about that?' said Kelly in amazement.

He told them what had been said at the meeting at the judge's house.

'The judge is cooking us up another job. He told Luther to keep out of sight until it was all arranged. I was to hang out in town and wait till the judge gave me the nod to fetch them in. But when we got to the saloon, it was full of drovers having a swell time. Luther asked why and they said two big cattle herds have just got into town and two more are due in a couple of days. By the middle of the week, the town would be full of buying and selling and money. Luther said he wasn't going to wait for no judge to come up with a scheme when he was sitting on banks full of money ready and waiting to be took. So he said he and the boys would go back to the old farm outside town and I would stay put as agreed. My job was to keep my ears open. Find out when the herds were due in, what brands were being herded, what days most sales would take place on, which bank was favoured by most owners. Then I'd report back and Luther would choose the time and the bank to hit.'

'Is that it?' said O'Leary.

'I swear to God,' said Kelly. 'Now what's going to happen to me?'

'I got choices,' said Tondu. 'I could lock you up until I got time to haul you off to Denver to face trial. Of course, I'd do what I could for you, but it might not be enough. However, if you were prepared to go on supplying this same calibre of information, I could pitch it stronger to the court. It would make enough difference to save your skin. Definite.'

'Meaning?' said Kelly uncertainly.

'You go back to the Four Aces, play more cards, drink more whiskey, tell Luther what he wants to know and let us know when he's going to hit the bank.'

'And which bank,' added Daco.

Kelly swallowed hard: 'He'd kill me if he finds out.'

'How's he going to find out?' said Daco. 'We won't tell him. And we'll make arrangements for the judge that'll keep him out of circulation. It's the best deal there is in town, John. What's it to be?'

Kelly hesitated, then conceded defeat. O'Leary removed the bullets from his six-gun before giving it back to him.

'Where do I report? I cain't hardly come here.'

'Just go on collecting information about who's selling and who's buying and keep feeding it to Luther. When you got something that might interest us, come to the judge's house,' said Daco.

'We got plans for the judge,' said O'Leary grimly.

'There's one more thing, John,' said Daco. 'You must have been with Luther up at that spread beyond Blackmill. A woman got shot.'

'That wasn't nothing to do with me,' said Kelly defensively.

'Tell me what happened.'

'It was Luther. He was after some feller who'd got him put away in jail.

Ward was his name. So we hit this Ward's farm. But he wasn't there, but his wife was. Luther said for us to put a scare in her. Boy, she put up some fight, I'll give her that. Anyhow, feller name of Newt Aldrich grabbed her, tied her to a chair. Then she got loose. She got hold of a knife and waved it about. Luther came in and damned if she didn't stick Newt in the hand before running out the door.'

Daco closed his eyes. But the picture was too vivid and he opened them again.

'Luther stood in the doorway, pulled out his gun, waited until she'd nearly made it to a sort of barn, then shot her.'

'In the back,' said Daco through gritted teeth.

Kelly stared at him until the penny dropped. The man Judge Prothero said was about the same height as Zeke was standing before him.

'By God, you're Ward!' he said in a scared voice.

'Get out!' said Daco.

11

When Kelly had gone, Tondu said:

'Think we can trust him?'

'I reckon he got the message,' said O'Leary. 'You boys put the fear of God in him one way or another. Turned his tripes to water.'

'Let's hope he stays good and scared,' said Tondu. 'But say, Sheriff, what did you have in mind when you said we'd be 'making arrangements' for the judge?'

'We can't let him roam free to go on cheating decent, hard-working folk, stealing their money from the bank and running them off their land. He's finished but he hasn't been stopped. He's in deep trouble if he only knew it. He ain't got the Hayes gang in his pocket no more; Luther has stopped listening to what he says. You heard Kelly: Luther's going his own way. And now he's got us breathing down his neck. I say we take the judge out of general circulation.'

'You're right,' said Tondu. 'But it's got to be done quiet. We don't want him kicking up a fuss before Luther makes his move, otherwise he'll scare him off. Best shut him away till we're good and ready to hand him over to the law.'

'Leave him to me, I got a scheme,' said O'Leary, with a gleam in his eye that hadn't been there for a long time. 'I'll get on it. Way I see it, you boys could do worse than ride out to Ike Barnard's old farm and keep an eye on how Luther and his boys are doing. We wouldn't want to lose track of them. Meantime, I'll handle the judge. I'll be at his house.'

'You do that,' said Tondu. 'When we've done spying, we'll join you there. We'll use his place as our base until we know which way Luther's going to jump.'

They rode off and Sheriff O'Leary headed for the judge's official residence, a solidly built, two-storey building standing on its own half-acre. The judge himself opened the door to the sheriff. It was late and the help had gone home.

'What do you mean by coming here at this time of night, O'Leary?' he barked.

He took the sheriff into his study and turned to face him. He found himself looking down the barrel of a six-shooter.

'What's this? The worm turning?' he sneered. 'Put that gun away and tell me what the problem is.'

With a show of unconcern, he sat down behind his desk. The sheriff followed him and slid open the drawer where he knew Prothero kept a small handgun. Judges make enemies. The ones that survive longest are the ones who take precautions.

That also holds true for sheriffs and that night O'Leary had the edge.

'Are you mad? What's got into you . . . ?'

'On your feet.'

When the judge refused to move, O'Leary prodded him with his gun. He kept it there while he steered him out of the study and along the passage. He stopped outside a door. It was the door to the cellar.

'Open it,' said O'Leary pleasantly.

The judge took a bunch of keys from his pocket and did as he was told. O'Leary took the whole bunch from him.

'You'll pay for this,' the judge snarled.

O'Leary's answer was to give him a shove with his boot. The judge staggered and just saved himself from falling down the steps that led to his well-furnished cellar where he stored his papers. It was also his strong room, where he kept his real wealth. The safe he'd let Luther see just contained spending money. Another, much larger safe bolted to a wall was where he kept cash, valuables and legal and financial documents. The door slammed behind him. He heard the key turn in the lock.

He shouted threats and beat on the door. He got no reaction.

He felt his way down the steps in the dark, and found the lamp and lit it. He sat at a scroll-top desk and tried to fathom what O'Leary was up to, but he saw no way through the puzzle. Eventually he dozed off. He slept fitfully but woke from a deep sleep when daylight filtered through the only window, high up in one wall. He'd had it secured with an iron grill to keep out ne'er-do-wells. He now regretted it, for it now made bars for his prison.

It wasn't the sun which had woken him, though it was already climbing up the sky, but the click of his gate latch. Mrs MacDonald! Saved! Frantically, he dragged his chair across to the window, piled half a dozen thick law books on it, climbed up and looked out at ground level. He saw a plump, middle-aged woman in long skirts and her second-best hat walking up the path to his front door. She was holding her key in her hand. He tapped the glass, trying to attract her attention. He called to her, but dared not make too much noise in case O'Leary heard. The man was clearly mad. And madmen are unpredictable. He called again and tapped but got no reaction.

Before she could put her key in the lock, he heard O'Leary open the door and wish her good morning. She sounded surprised to see him.

'That's good,' he thought, 'she suspects something's wrong.'

Then he heard the sheriff say:

'The judge was called away unexpected. He told me to tell you he'd be gone for a few days. He says there's nothing he wants you to do. No cleaning or cooking. He'll let you know when he gets back.'

'Men!' snorted Mrs MacDonald. 'There's always something to do in a house this size. With him not here, I'd have a free hand — '

'Sorry, ma'am, but he said most particular that he didn't want you to do anything. 'That woman works a sight too hard', he said. 'She deserves a rest'. And he left this envelope. A bonus, he said.'

Mrs MacDonald's tone softened.

'Well it's nice to be appreciated, I'm sure.'

'Take it, sounds like you got yourself a holiday. Make the most of it.'

Mollified, Mrs MacDonald turned and walked back towards the gate.

The judge tapped on the window pane again, and called as loudly as he dared. But still not hearing, she carefully closed the gate behind her and was gone.

Moments later, the door at the top of the steps opened and O'Leary set a plate on the ground.

'Breakfast,' he announced and before the judge could move or say a word, he shut the door again and locked it.

The judge climbed the steps and inspected the plate. There was a hunk of bread and several thick slices of cured meat. The smell reminded him that he was hungry.

He took the plate down to the cellar

and, using his desk as a table, wolfed down his breakfast. He immediately began to feel better. The bacon had been good, though too salty for his taste, and the bread had been dry.

He examined his surroundings inch by inch. The high window was sealed: even if he broke the glass, the bars would stop him. There was no way out through the walls, which were below ground-level. His only chance was the door at the top of the stairs. It was made of oak too thick to break down and hard enough to blunt an axe, even if he'd had one. Maybe he could pick the lock. Felons of low intelligence had often come before him in court. Some of them regularly picked locks in the course of their crimes. If they could do it, so could an educated, smart man like himself. He went back down the steps and started hunting for something to use as a picklock. He was still looking when the door opened and O'Leary called down to him.

'Chow time!'

He set another plate on the ground and locked the door again.

The judge was amazed. It seemed no time since he'd eaten breakfast. But both his watch and his stomach confirmed that the hours had indeed fled by. He took the plate down to his chair where he started to eat.

It was the same fare. Chewy salt bacon and dry bread. At least O'Leary, though the man was off his head, had remembered to feed him.

So far.

Suddenly he felt weary. He had slept badly the previous night and a full stomach made him drowsy.

When he woke, he looked at his watch. It had stopped. He had forgotten to wind it. But the light was dimmer now and he guessed it must now be late afternoon. Then he was suddenly aware that he was thirsty. He was also hot. But the thirst was worse. He hadn't had anything to drink for nigh on twelve hours and the salt in the bacon wasn't helping.

He'd heard that sucking on a pebble brought relief. But he didn't have a pebble. He found a small glass paperweight and used that instead. He sucked on it. It helped. But not for long.

Then the door opened again and O'Leary called down: 'Supper!'

This time, the judge was too quick for him. Before the sheriff shut the door, he shouted up: 'You've forgotten to give me anything to drink!'

'I didn't forget,' said O'Leary. 'You never asked. The grub's free. Any drinks you order you pay for. What do you want? Beer?'

'Beer would be fine,' said the judge. The image of a frothing glass rose up in his mind.

'Payment in advance,' said O'Leary stonily.

'How much?' asked the judge, feverishly reaching for his wallet, frantic at the thought that the sheriff would lock him in again without giving him anything to drink.

'Two hundred and fifty dollars,' said

O'Leary in the same flat voice.

'What?' exclaimed the judge. 'That's ridiculous!'

'Suit yourself,' said O'Leary and he slammed the door on his prisoner.

The judge skinned his knuckles on the oak. He shouted himself hoarse before he realized he was wasting his time. He made his way back down the steps. He tried to eat, but his mouth was too dry for him to swallow. He spent a second uncomfortable night.

When O'Leary brought breakfast next morning, the judge had drunk nothing for what seemed like days. His tongue was like hard leather. He could hardly speak.

'Do you want to eat or not?' the sheriff called down the steps.

'Got to have something to drink', the judge croaked, as he started up the steps.

'What do you want? Beer?

'No. Is there something cheaper? Water will be fine.'

'All drinks is the same price. Water,

beer, rye whiskey, there's all sorts of drinks.'

'You can't do this to me!' said the judge furiously.

'I make the rules here, Judge. You're in my court now. So, do you want a drink or don't you? Come on, I got things to do. You're wasting my time.'

There was no sense in antagonizing O'Leary. He had the whip hand. Besides, he had to have something to drink. His mouth felt like lizard skin. How long was it a man could go without water? Three days? Five? He couldn't remember. But it wasn't as long as a man could go without eating.

'All right,' he said. 'Give me water. Wait. I'll go get the money.'

The judge shambled down the steps, opened the safe with the key on his watch chain, took out five fifty-dollar bills, closed the safe and climbed wearily back up the steps.

'Here's the money,' he said.

'That ain't enough. The price has gone up. Today all drinks are five

137

hundred dollars.'

'For pity's sake . . . ' started the judge before the door slammed in his face.

At chow time, he was desperate and begged for water. He held out his five hundred dollars, only to be told the price was now a thousand.

'All right,' he said in a dry, papery whimper. 'Wait.'

He fetched more money. When he reached the top of the steps, O'Leary held out one hand for the money and with the other gave him a tall glass of water.

'Drink it slow, Judge. Make it last. Here's your receipt. Remember, I never forced you to buy any drinks. Next time, if you want more, have the money ready. And don't forget, every time the price doubles.'

The judge had never tasted any drink more satisfying than that pure, clean, cool water. He rolled it round his mouth, letting it wash over his tongue, his teeth, the inside of his cheeks, then swallowed it as if it was fine French brandy. He handed back the glass.

'How long is this going on for?'

'Not long at the rate the price of water's going up, Judge. But I was forgetting, there's no man knows more than you about the price of water. People pay for it with their farms, their dreams, their future. You sure are a thirsty man. You'll have to keep shelling out for it until there's no money left in that safe of yours. And when you run out of cash, since I'm a reasonable sort of man, I'll accept land deeds instead. But only the deeds to the farms of the men you fleeced. Then when the folks from back East who're going to build us a dam full of water — cain't you just picture all that water? — come along, we'll set up a company offering all the land they want, the same land you bought cheap so you could sell it dear.'

'You won't get away with this, O'Leary,' the judge snarled. 'I'll see you in hell before that day! But first I'll see you in court. You'll be arraigned for false imprisonment, extortion, larceny, torture — '

'I'll be back,' smiled the sheriff. 'So have the two thousand ready. Don't make me wait again.'

And he slammed the door, leaving the judge to his thoughts.

12

Since Tondu and Daco saw it last, Ike
Barnard's farm hadn't been neatened
up, nor were there any fresh signs that
it was occupied. But there was an
indefinable sense of occupation, which
Tondu picked up more readily than
Daco. He was always at home in the
open air, camping on a mountain,
watching the first sun rosying the tops
of high sierras, washing in a mountain
stream. What told him that there were
men about was the absence of the usual
rustle and scuffle of God's night
creatures as they went looking for food.
The quiet wasn't natural.

But it was Daco who saw the gleam
of moonlight on gun metal.

'They set a guard,' he whispered.
'There. Just by that broken-down gate.'

They'd left their horses tethered
among rocks at a safe distance.

Treading quietly, they turned and started back they way they'd come. When they reached the rocks and could talk without fear of giving the alarm, Tondu produced his pipe and Daco rolled himself a smoke.

'Looks like Kelly was telling the truth,' said Tondu. 'Luther's waiting till he gets a signal to make a move.'

'And going by what he said,' said Daco, 'Luther's gang must be down to about six men. Take Kelly away, and the sentry on duty, that leaves just four of them in the house: Luther, Zeke and two more.'

'The odds are getting better all the time.'

'We could shorten them more by taking the guard out of the reckoning.'

'Why not?' grinned Tondu. 'It would be something to do.'

They smoked for a while longer in silence then headed back towards the farm.

The guard was still in the same place. He hadn't moved.

But he wasn't asleep and he brought his gun up when Daco suddenly emerged from nowhere.

'Couldn't sleep,' he mumbled indistinctly. 'Came to relieve you.'

'Is that you, Clip?' said the guard.

Tondu was in position, behind him, a yard or two away.

Daco yawned and said something that could have been 'Yup'.

The guard relaxed. As he did so, Tondu tapped him on the shoulder. The guard turned instinctively. Tondu hit him on the jaw. The guard went down like a puppet who's had his strings cut. Between them, they dragged the unconscious man back to their rocks and tied him across Daco's saddle. Then they rode slowly back to town. They met no one on the road, and the streets of Bridgend were deserted at this hour.

Light showed in the sheriff's office. It was not locked and it wasn't empty either.

'I came to report my hat got stole,' said Kenny Cole. 'Where'sh sheriff?'

He peered at Tondu and said suspiciously: 'You ain't the sheriff.' Then his face lit up.

'My fren' Jawbones!' he said happily to Tondu. 'And Taters O'Hara! Let's go have a drink, boys!'

Daco and Tondu carried the still unconscious guard to the door of the cell. Daco fetched the keys.

'Who's the corpse?' said Kenny. 'Looks like he had his hat stole too.'

'Sure did,' said Tondu while Daco took the keys from the hook on the wall. 'Must be some crazy cowboy going round stealing hats.'

'That a fact?' said Kenny blearily.

'Step inside, Kenny,' said Daco as he unlocked the cell door. 'I got a job for you. I want you to stay with Harry No-Hat here. Look after him.'

'Glad to oblige boys,' said Kenny who made straight for the cot, stretched out and began snoring at once.

Daco and Tondu lugged the unconscious guard into the cell after him, blew out the lamp, locked the outer door and made for Judge Prothero's house. O'Leary filled them in, explaining what he'd done with the judge. Daco smiled. He especially liked the idea of feeding him salt bacon. The man would wake up with a raging thirst. They helped themselves to victuals they found in the kitchen — the judge did himself well — and spent what was left of the night comfortably.

Next morning, after feeding his prisoner, the sheriff let Kenny Cole out of jail but kept Luther's man locked up. Then he patrolled through town, as he did most days. He called in at the Four Aces for a beer. John Kelly was there. O'Leary caught his eye. Kelly shook his head: nothing to report.

Over the next couple of days while Judge Prothero's money vanished from his safe at an increasing rate, O'Leary ran a regular eye over the cattle pens down at Newbridge Fields, which were filling up fast. From time to time, he glimpsed John Kelly who was also watching beef and money changing hands. Daco and Tondu kept an eye on him and tracked him when he went back to Ike Barnard's farm each night to report to Luther. No more sentries were posted to guard the place. Kelly told them that since the sentry had disappeared, Luther's men weren't keen on doing the job.

O'Leary knew some of the cattlemen and most of the buyers who came every year by railroad to buy their quota of steers. He approached a few of the drovers, told them he suspected that trouble was brewing and asked if they'd lend a hand to stop it. One or two jibbed, but most said they'd be glad to join in if it meant putting a gang of jayhawkers behind bars. Marauders had cost them a lot of money over the years.

The day the main sale started, the sheriff, Daco and Tondu held a conference.

'What's the latest from Kelly?' asked Daco.

'He's been a good boy. Does what he's told. He reckons Luther's started to fret. He ain't the type to sit around. Most of the money that's heading for banks will get paid in by the end of today. Kelly reckons Luther will hit the bank tomorrow.'

'Which one?' asked Tondu.

'Dawson's,' said the sheriff. 'There's three banks in town. Dawson's, down near the Fields, the First Ensign on Main Street, and the Sovereign, away on the far side of town. Dawson's is the first port of call every year and Cousins, the manager, agrees that if anyone is going to be hit, it's him.'

'Does Dawson's employ its own guards?' asked Tondu.

'A couple, but as a rule Cousins recruits another two or three guns at this time of year. It's his most busy time and he always feels he's a target. He's got some lined up for tomorrow.'

'Should be enough,' said Tondu. 'Looks like we won't be needing those extra cattlemen after all.'

'Still,' said O'Leary, 'they might come in handy.'

After dark, Daco and Tondu rode out to Ike Barnard's farm. It looked as deserted as ever but even Daco could see now that it wasn't. Luther and his men were still there, all right. But, when they got back to town, Kelly wasn't in the Four Aces or any place else where they looked.

'Must have gone to report back,' said Tondu. 'Luther's now got all he needs to know, which bank to raid, what security there is and the rest of it. He won't wait any longer. It's on for tomorrow.'

'I'll go and put the word about,' said O'Leary. 'But first, I got to ask the judge if he wants another drink to go with his hard-boiled eggs and dry biscuit.'

At first, the judge had put up resistance. He had refused to buy water. But by day three, his parched body was crying out for something to drink and he weakened. When the sheriff brought his breakfast, he was standing with the two thousand dollars in bills ready in his hand.

'Rightly speaking, the price goes up

148

every mealtime whether you buy a drink or not. But I'll make it easy for you. Gimme the two thousand and I'll give you water. Though not quite as much.'

Instead of the usual tumbler, he brought one of the judge's dainty wineglasses. While the prisoner drank it as slowly as he could manage, O'Leary wrote him a new receipt to add to the others he'd given for the drinks he'd paid for, then slammed the door shut.

The next morning, the judge was light-headed. He'd lost track of time and the price of a glass of water, but he thought it must be in the tens of thousands. He didn't have thousands — he couldn't raise it. The sheriff settled for what he had, which was nigh on eight thousand. It was all the cash he had left. So instead of dollar bills the sheriff started accepting deeds for the land the judge had bought up cheap. Before he got his drink, he had to sign away his ownership of one, then two, then four, then eight properties and transfer them back to their rightful owners.

The day Luther was expected to hold up the bank, he ran out of deeds. The sheriff brought him a royal feast and three jugs of water.

'Chow! And it's on the house,' he called, before he slammed the door.

* * *

That same morning, Daco and Tondu had hit the trail early, before the town was up and stirring. They left their horses in the cluster of rocks and got as near to the farm as they dared. The only visible signs of life were the occasional predator flying high in the sky and the wind raising dust into swirls.

It was still quiet at noon, when the sun was high, and when it began to head down for the horizon, it went on being quiet.

'What's Luther waiting for?' asked Daco. 'Maybe they've cleared out? Maybe we're missing the action!'

'They ain't gone no place,' said Tondu. 'They're still in there.'

Around four in the afternoon, a solitary rider left the farm and headed for the road to Bridgend. He was wearing a long-skirted cattleman's coat and a broad-brimmed hat. He was in no hurry.

'Which one is that?' said Tondu.

'Could be any of 'em,' said Daco. 'But we'd better see where he goes. Toss you for it.'

Tondu lost. While he stayed to watch the farm, Daco followed the solitary rider who did not seem in any sort of hurry.

It was just after five o'clock.

13

Arthur Cousins glanced up at the clock in his office. Quarter past five. He had managed Dawson's Bank in Bridgend for twenty years. He was a big man but at fifty he was losing his hair and running to fat. He was at the time of life where a man found that clothes he doesn't wear for a month or two shrink all by themselves on their hangers in the closet. 'Too much time spent behind a damned desk, that's the root of it,' he would say with a shrug. He had regular habits and an orderly mind, and he made sure his bank ran efficiently. He treated his employees firmly but fairly, was good with clients and could account for every cent that came in and went out though his doors.

He looked up again at the clock. Another ten minutes and he could close the shutters, lock the door and go home. The bank had had a good day, with sellers from the cattle fair queuing up to put their cash in his vaults. At home, an agreeable wife who fed him well, two healthy children and a dog were waiting. Arthur Cousins liked his life.

Baynes, his head cashier, knocked on his door.

'Client to see you, Mr Cousins, sir. Shall I show him in?'

'Is he wanting to deposit cash or is he asking for a loan?'

'He says he's just sold a herd, so I guess he's a depositor.'

It was now twenty-five past the hour. It was too late in the day to start discussing a loan for a new customer but still early enough to accept a deposit.

'Show him in,' said Mr Cousins.

He looked up from the letters he'd dictated earlier and saw a man, not tall, with dark eyes and dark stubble on his chin. He was wearing a long-skirted cattleman's coat and a broad-brimmed hat. Mr Cousins gestured to a chair and the man sat down. The skirts of his coat hung down to the floor. Calmly, he produced a six-gun from a pocket of the coat and enjoyed the expression on the bank manager's face when he saw it pointing at him.

'Here's what you do. You go to your office door but no further. From there you tell your people it's time to go home. You will say you have me to deal with and papers to check. A whole bunch of papers. It'll take you some time, so no one's expecting you. Send one of them to your house to say they're not to wait on dinner. You'll be working very late, so best not to stay up for you. We don't want to be interrupted by anyone coming to see where you're at and why you ain't home. That way no one gets hurt. And stand your security down. When they've all gone, you close the shutters, lock the door, come back here and give me the key. I'll have you covered all the way. So do what you're told and don't try to be a hero.'

'Are you . . . do you intend to, er, rob the bank?'

'That's the idea,' said Zeke Goodwin. 'Stay here and keep talking till it's 5.30 on the clock. Ask me questions, tell me about the weather, just keep talking. Somebody might come in. Make it look natural.'

All Mr Cousins could think of to say was: 'Is this the first bank you ever robbed?'

Zeke looked at the clock on the wall.

'Go tell them now. And don't forget, I'll have a gun on you all the way.'

Mr Cousins got to his feet, wiped his clammy hands on the front of his jacket and went out to tell his staff they could go home. They looked up, surprised. This wasn't like the boss. He liked to see their desks tidy before they left for the day. But they didn't argue and reached for their coats. Then Baynes said:

'What about the man from the Fields, sir, with cash to deposit? Would you like me to stay until he's off the premises?'

'No,' said Mr Cousins sharply. 'I'll need some time with him. A complicated deposit. I'll let him out when we're good and done. I repeat: you may go.'

Then he added, to take the harsh edge off what he'd just said: 'Everyone's worked hard today. Letting staff go a little early is good for morale, Baynes. You should remember that for when you get to be a manager. I'll see you in the morning.'

'Shaw, the night security man, will be here soon, so I guess it's all right.'

'Tell him he can stay home too. Nothing's going to happen to the bank tonight. If we haven't been hit by now, it's not going to happen. I expect I'll be here most of the night.'

When Baynes expressed surprise, Mr Cousins told him to do what he was told. From his office door, he watched Baynes, his two tellers, the hired guards and the office boy file out. When the last had gone, Mr Cousins lowered the shutters, locked the door and returned to his office. There the man had removed his cattleman's coat but his broad-brimmed hat was still on his head. The man tied him to his chair and stuffed a gag in his mouth.

★ ★ ★

Daco had taken up a position in the alley opposite Dawson's Bank, between Mackenzie's tack shop and the town's tooth-puller's office. He leaned against the wall, rolled himself a smoke. When he'd smoked it, he rolled another.

He saw the man in the cattleman's coat walk into Dawson's Bank a few minutes before it was due to close. Minutes later, the bank staff in their sober suits left, along with the armed security guards. The man with the cattleman's coat did not come out. The shutters came down and the manager, after looking nervously up and down the street, locked himself inside.

Nothing happened for half an hour. By then, Daco knew what was going down. Luther's boys would arrive after dark. They wouldn't need to break in; they would walk straight through the front door of the bank which would be opened from inside. By then, Cousins, the manager would have been persuaded to open the strong room door.

When the half hour was up, he left his post and sauntered round to the back of the bank. There was just one ground floor window. Cautiously he sidled along the wall until he was able to risk a peek. It was barred on the inside. The room was empty. But there were papers on the floor and a chair had been overturned. Signs of a struggle.

He returned to his post by the tooth-puller's house of pain and waited a while longer. He did some more thinking. Nothing was going to happen before dark and very likely not for hours after that. He figured Luther wouldn't pull out of the farm until all Bridgend was tucked up in bed and fast asleep. There was nothing to be gained by hanging around. He decided to ride out and put Tondu in the picture.

As he rode, he thought some more. There were two choices: they could follow when the gang set out for town, or they could leave first and lay on a welcome for them.

'I reckon we leave first,' said Tondu when Daco put it to him. 'The bank is where the action's going to happen. We can use the time to scout round and work out how we're going to play it.'

'I was thinking we could get the sheriff on side. He said he could call on volunteers among the cattlemen.'

And so the battle plan was laid.

★ ★ ★

Judge Prothero woke from a deep nap with a start. He was instantly alert. He was aware of feeling better than he had for days. He had thrown off not only the exhaustion but that feeling of helplessness. The last meal O'Leary had set down for him and a couple of hours of solid rest had set him up. He was ready for a fight.

The house was quiet. He waited. Time passed, which he spent thinking about how the sheriff had tried to ruin him and how he could put things to right. First, he'd take his star away and have him locked up until he could stand trial for embezzlement. Then he'd make him reveal where he'd hidden the money and third, he'd recover the deeds to the properties he'd bought. Signatures extracted under duress were not valid in law. He'd throw the book at O'Leary who wouldn't see the blue skies of freedom this side of the Day of Judgement!

He was suddenly aware that he was hungry again but also that O'Leary had not dumped his tray on the top step in the usual way. He waited a while, then climbed the stairs and beat on the door to attract attention. To his amazement, it swung open. A stroke of luck! His jailer had forgotten to lock it! He quickly stepped out into the passageway and listened. Nothing. The house was silent as the grave. There was nobody there. Carefully he made his way to his office, found a weapon in the shape of a heavy walking stick, and stood by his desk. He needed to think about what to do.

He hadn't got far with his plans when he heard the sound of the latch of his garden gate. It must be O'Leary coming back. He gripped his stick tightly, ready to attack or defend as the case may be. A key was inserted in the lock of his front door. Holding his breath, he moved quickly out of his office and looked down the passage. Expecting to see the sheriff, he tightened his grip on his stick and braced himself for action. Then he heard Mrs MacDonald humming a hymn tune. She looked up and let out a shriek.

'Is that you, Judge?' she said.

'Who were you expecting?'

'Oh, you gave me a fright! I knew you were back, Sheriff told me, so I came to see if there was anything I could do. But just look at the state of you!'

The judge glanced into a mirror on the wall. The face that stared back at him was unshaven and unwashed and his clothes were crumpled. He realized he didn't smell good either.

'Never mind,' said Mrs MacDonald. 'Anything is forgiven a man as good as yourself! 'Tis a fine thing you have done, to be sure!'

And she went off, still clucking, to lay out a change of clothes for him.

The judge assumed that the 'fine thing' was giving her a holiday. He smiled grimly. He washed and climbed into the clothes she'd laid out. Ten minutes later, he walked into Kyle Martin's barber's shop for a shave. Kyle wouldn't let him pay, saying it was the least he could do for 'a true benefactor of Ogmore County'.

Judge Prothero's next stop was Maisie Kinnear's diner. He got the same welcome there, the same refusal to let him to pay for his meat and gravy. As he lingered over a second cup of coffee, his eye was attracted by the

162

headline in the town's twice-weekly paper, the *Bridgend Advertiser*, fresh out that morning. Printed in large, bold letters, it read: 'Benefactor of the Century?' He reached for it and started reading the story under the headline:

The Advertiser eats humble pie and is glad to!

We can today reveal the truth behind the operations of the faceless company which has for over six months, been buying up farms and homesteads in Peace Valley which will be flooded when the new dam gets built.

As our regular readers know, the Advertiser has campaigned long and hard against what we honestly believed was a sinister consortium of banks, speculators and profiteers. We accused the company of buying up land at rock-bottom prices and forcing homesteaders off their farms with a view to assembling a portfolio of properties which it would sell at a fat profit when the authorities finally acquire

163

the land for flooding.

We complained, we railed, we cried fraud!

BUT WE WERE WRONG!

And now we are glad to put the record straight.

There was no sinister company interested only in profit.

We can reveal that the consortium was in fact one man who has worked selflessly and untiringly for the people for thirty years and now crowns his life's work by giving Peace Valley, free of charge and for ever, to the folks who once owned it. When the land is bought, they alone will reap the benefit.

And the name of this great public benefactor?

Judge Prothero!

The Great Benefactor choked on his coffee. O'Leary had boxed him into a corner! His private affairs were now a matter of public record. If he went to law to get the sheriff to return his money, people would wonder how, on his modest salary, he could have come by such a fortune honestly. And if he tried to get the deeds reassigned to himself, everyone would know that what the *Advertiser* had suspected had been true all along and that he was the faceless profiteer its campaign had denounced.

As he walked home, people he didn't know came up to him, expressing their gratitude and wanting to shake his hand. But the judge didn't linger and he barely spoke.

'Strange way of carrying on,' said Mrs Tom Boot, the blacksmith's wife. 'You'd think he could have stopped and acted more pleasant.'

'Well,' said Pastor Mason, 'I guess there's only so much a man can take of folks having a good opinion of him.'

'Yes, that must be it,' said Mrs Tom Boot.

14

Arthur Cousins proved to be a stubborn as well as a loyal servant of Dawson's Bank. Another man might have said it wasn't his bank that was being robbed, not his money that was being stolen, so why put up a fight to save what wasn't his? The fact was, he didn't so much fear as despise this thief who could walk into his office, hide behind a gun and take money for which decent men had worked hard to earn. So when Zeke told him to open the strong room, he shook his head.

Zeke punched him so hard that the chair he was tied to fell hard against his desk before hitting the floor. A shower of his papers cascaded over him.

Zeke stood over him and repeated his order.

Again Arthur Cousins shook his head in refusal.

Zeke kicked him once in the ribs and once in the head.

Mr Cousins started to bleed.

'Don't be a fool to yourself, Mr Manager,' said Zeke mildly. 'You're going to do what I say sooner or later. You'll get tired of being beat up. You ain't used to it. You can't take it. Might as well settle your mind to it now and save yourself a lot of pain.'

He made his point by kicking Cousins savagely in the ribs once more. The bank manager gasped in agony. He was sure he'd felt something break.

Zeke yanked his chair upright and slapped him hard across the mouth. Then he held his nose in a tight grip. After no more than thirty seconds, Cousins' eyes bulged and he started thrashing wildly. With a gag in his mouth and a thumb over his nose he couldn't breathe. Zeke released his grip and the bank manager started gulping air through his nostrils. With each intake, he felt a tearing pain in his ribs. Zeke repeated the medicine, this time holding his man's nose until he felt he was about to pass out. When Cousins' breathing had returned almost to normal and his colour had changed from blue to pink, Zeke rolled and lit a cigarette and blew smoke in his face. Cousins coughed. The stabbing pain in his ribs was agony. How he hated this bully!

'Had enough?'

Cousins nodded.

Zeke removed the gag from his mouth, untied him and yanked him to his feet.

'Where's the vault?' he snarled.

'Cellar,' gasped Cousins.

With Zeke's gun in his back, he staggered to another door discreetly hidden behind the head cashier's high desk. From his belt he selected a key and opened it. He led the way down a short flight of steps to a bare, stone-flagged, brick-walled room. Set in one wall was a massive ceiling-to-floor iron door fitted with a combination lock. It was the strongroom. He wiped his sweating hands on the front of his jacket and started turning the tumblers until there was a click and he was able to swing the door open.

Despite the rough-housing he'd been given, Cousins was still game. He stepped aside to let Zeke pass. It was part of his plan. The minute Zeke was inside, he'd slam the door on him and lock it. Then he'd go back upstairs and raise the alarm . . .

But the moment the door opened, Zeke turned and caught him with a fierce right to the jaw.

The bank manager sagged and went down without a sound.

Without giving him another glance, Zeke gave his attention to the contents of the strongroom. He saw bags of gold dust brought in by miners from their claims in the hills of Ogmore County and wads of bills in neatly labelled boxes.

There was enough money here to make even Luther happy, he thought. He left the gold untouched. Gold is pretty, but it's also heavy, awkward to carry and hard to convert into cash, for the money-changers were no more honest than the thieves who brought it to them. On a shelf was a pile of large canvas bags stamped 'Dawson's Bank'. He opened the labelled boxes and began transferring the bills. When the first bag was full, he began a second. In all, he filled five bags. He had no idea how much money there was in those five bags, but it had to be a lot.

From time to time, he stopped to listen for signs of trouble. But all was quiet.

When Arthur Cousins began to groan, Zeke tied his feet and bound his hands behind his back. He put the gag back in his mouth, then he went upstairs and peered through the shutters. It was getting dark. The street outside was empty. He returned to the manager's office and levered the iron bars from the window. When he'd finished, he drew the curtains and lit the lamp so that everything would look normal to anyone who might pass by. The manager was supposed to be working. He couldn't work in the dark.

After hauling all five bags to the front door, he sat down to wait.

He took out the makings and smoked a cigarette.

He felt he'd earned it.

The hands on the clock in Arthur Cousins' office declared the time to be close on ten o'clock.

★   ★   ★

The cattlemen had delivered as promised. Ten handy-looking cowpokes with guns strapped to their thighs and the light of battle in their eyes had gathered in Sheriff O'Leary's office.

Leaving Daco to watch the bank, Tondu joined them and laid out the plan.

'They've got a man inside,' he said. 'Been there since the bank closed. By now, he'll have made the manager open the safe and put the contents by the front door, in bags, for the quick getaway. So this is no ordinary stick-up.

No staff to deal with, no customers to make things complicated, the money's already been stolen. It's a collection. They'll have come and gone before anyone cottons on to what's happening.'

'We got two options,' he went on. 'We can go in now, take the man who's in there and wait inside for Luther and his boys to walk in. Then we can take them all down. Or we wait outside and collar them as they're getting away. Daco and I been giving it some thought. We reckon the second is the best option. If we go in shooting, their man will shoot back. There'd be a commotion, town folks would come out in their night-shirts to see what all the fuss is all about, we'd lose the element of surprise and Luther and his boys will hightail it out of town before we get a chance at them.'

The sheriff backed him up and the improvised posse agreed.

'But we'll need to have horses down there. If Luther arrives, smells a rat and takes off, we'll need to be able to go after him.'

They moved off to set the trap.

From his post by the tooth-puller's office, Daco reported that all had been quiet as mice.

Tondu and the sheriff positioned their men strategically at the mouths of dark alleys, behind water butts and whatever cover was available. One of the cowboys corralled the horses in a cattle pen down at the Fields and stayed with them, ready to bring them up fast if needed. Tondu gave orders that there was to be no shooting until he gave the word. As long as they kept their heads down and gave Luther's marauders nothing to make them suspect they were walking into a trap, the fight would be over before it started and nobody would get hurt.

They settled down to wait.

It was a fine night but ragged clouds flitted at intervals across the face of the moon, spreading curtains of deep shadow and then suddenly snatching them away again. Time passed slowly and it was well past midnight when Daco caught the first sounds of approaching horses. The jayhawkers had wrapped cloths around their horses' hoofs to muffle the sound. Four riders pulled up at the bank and tethered their mounts to the hitching rail. The light was strong enough now for Daco to make out his mustang and Tondu's black stallion. One man tethered a riderless horse with the others: he assumed it was for the robber inside.

In a flicker of moonlight between passing clouds, the watching men saw them move quietly to the door of the bank. As they approached, it opened. Two men went in, two stayed outside with guns in their fists. One was Luther Hayes. A moment later, the two who had gone in emerged with a sack in each hand. A third man in a broad-brimmed hat came out holding another sack. Five sacks in all. They were about to hang them on their saddles and ride off into the night when Tondu gave the word.

Suddenly, there were men everywhere.

'It's no good Luther!' shouted Tondu. 'We've got the place surrounded. Throw down your guns!'

Luther's answer was to turn and dive straight back inside the bank. His men followed in a hail of bullets. Clip Curtz got hit twice and died instantly. Rees, shot in the shoulder, went down and did not try to get up. But Zeke and Kelly made it in safely. The door slammed shut. There was a sound of breaking glass. Tondu shouted to his men to take cover. The barrel of a gun poked out through the shutters over the front windows. He shouted a warning, but the shots found one target. One of the cowboys was hit and fell in a heap.

'Damn!' said Sheriff O'Leary. 'Looks like we got a regular siege on our hands after all.'

'What happens next?' asked Frenchy Durand, foreman of the Lazy T herd. 'Do we sit here and starve them out?'

'Negotiations,' said Daco. 'They got a hostage. They'll use him as a bargaining counter. His freedom in exchange for a safe passage.'

'There's also one of their men down,' said Tondu. 'Looks like he's losing a lot of blood.'

'Not that Luther will care,' said Daco.

'What's round the back of the bank? Can they escape that way?' asked Tondu.

'It's mostly wall with a window on the ground floor. The manager's office. It's secure. It's got bars over it. Still, if we can get near enough, we might get to see what they're up to. You stay here, Tondu, and take care of any parleying that needs doing.'

Waiting for a patch of shadow, Daco set off at a crouching run. He rounded the end of the bank, began to sidle along the back wall and stopped.

A man was climbing out of the window.

Daco called himself all sorts of names for not anticipating this. Luther was too wily to let himself get into any fix where there wasn't a back way out. His man had been inside the building for six, seven hours. That gave him plenty of time not just to get the money out of the safe and into bags, but also to remove the bars from the back window.

Daco stepped away from the wall and barked: 'Hold it right there!'

The man had one leg over the sill and was holding a bag in his right hand. The light of the oil-lamp inside the room was strong enough for Daco to recognize Zeke Goodwin.

Zeke dropped the bag on the ground and held up both hands.

'Throw down your gun,' said Daco. 'Good. Now start walking towards me, nice and slow, and don't try anything.'

He had spoken softly and Zeke had given no indication that anything was wrong.

He heard Tondu sing out: 'Luther! It's the end of the road. Best call it a day. Come on out before we come in!'

Daco heard no reply. Keeping a wary eye on the lighted window, he watched while Zeke came towards him, hands in the air. He wondered why Zeke had kept so quiet, done nothing to tip Luther off to the fact that their escape route was cut.

The barrel of a gun, rammed against his back, told him why. Zeke hadn't been first man out.

'Well, well,' said Luther in a low, menacing voice, reaching forward and taking Daco's gun from him. 'If it isn't my old friend Ward! I been looking for you all over, Sergeant, to chat about old times and how you gave me up to army justice. And now you've come to me and we can have that little chat here and now!'

'Cut that out!' said Zeke in an urgent whisper. 'We ain't got time for it. We got to go, without attracting attention. Shoot Ward and you'll have a posse here in less time than it takes to spit!'

'The man's right, Ward! I can't get my satisfaction now. But it'll keep for when we meet up again!'

He holstered his gun, clenched both fists and took a half a dozen steps forward.

All the while Luther was talking, Daco had a picture of Ginny running down the path and Luther letting her almost reach cover before coolly, murderously, shooting her in the back. He saw the bullet burst into her flesh, he felt the hurt she had felt. So when Luther, half a foot taller and a good sight brawnier, started to shape up, he saw red.

As Luther swung, he dived and came up inside his guard with a right that carried all his strength, all his weight and all his hate. Luther gasped, his chin dropped onto an uppercut which missed his chin but got him on the Adam's apple. The big man made a choking noise and holding both hands to his throat toppled backwards into the dust where he fought for breath.

As Daco moved to follow up, something hit him on the back of the head. He staggered but did not go down until Zeke hit him a second time. Snapping an order to Kelly who disappeared into the darkness, Zeke waited until Luther's breathing began to return to normal. Luther's first thought was to put a bullet in Daco. It wasn't the slow punishment he'd had in mind, but it would do. But Zeke took his gun off him.

'I told you, Luther. No noise. Do you want to get us put back behind bars or killed? Just stay quiet till Kelly gets back. I sent him to find us something to ride.'

From the front of the bank, they heard Tondu giving out an ultimatum.

Then Zeke heard a rustle of approaching footsteps in the dark. He raised his gun then lowered it.

'I got us some horses. A cowpoke was guarding a dozen head down by the river, all saddled up and ready to go. They're ours for the taking. Let's go. The guard won't give us no trouble — he's out cold.'

While Luther still wheezed and whispered threats over the unconscious Daco, warning him to keep watching his back, Zeke shouldered two bags and passed a third to John Kelly. Three bags weren't as good as five, but he knew they were full.

They moved quietly towards the Fields where Kelly had found the horses.

At the front of the bank, Tondu, losing patience, gave the order for the shooting to start. When no one shot back, he knew there was no one home and the chase was on.

15

For Zeke Goodwin it was plain as day. Only Judge Prothero could have worked out that they'd very likely cut him out and try to rob a bank without his help. Who else could have passed the word to the law? But he didn't see where Ward and his big friend fitted in. As they went to get the horses, he questioned Kelly who again swore the judge had not once tried to contact him all the time he'd been at the Four Aces. The conclusion was obvious: Judge Prothero was not working on another job for them, like he said he would, nor was he looking after their interests. The opposite. He wanted them dead so they couldn't talk. Luther and his boys knew too much.

Zeke shared his thoughts with Luther.

'The lowdown rat! And him a judge!' the big man whispered hoarsely. 'Yeah, it figures.'

'What say we pay a call?' said Zeke.

'I thought we're supposed to be getting out of here, urgent, pronto or sooner,' said Kelly.

'He owes us money and this time we're going to get it,' replied Zeke. 'It won't take long. Nobody'll think we'd been dumb enough to hang around in town. The judge's house is the last place they'll start looking for us. When we've spoken with His Honour, we scout round and see which way the posse went, then we take off in the opposite direction.'

Judge Prothero came to the door in his nightshirt over which he'd hurriedly put on a pair of pants. Before he could say a word, Luther took him by the throat and three parts carried him along the passage. He stopped outside the judge's study. Zeke followed. Kelly stayed outside with orders to watch out for trouble.

'We come for our money,' rasped Luther.

After pointing Luther in the right

direction, Zeke always let him do the talking. He was a very persuasive talker.

'We ain't thinking of staying,' Luther went on. 'So jest give us our money and we'll be on our way.'

'There's no money,' spluttered the judge. 'I was cleaned out.'

'Who cleaned you out?' asked Zeke.

'O'Leary. He was on to me. Locked me up and cleaned me out.'

'I don't believe you,' said Zeke.

'I'll show you,' said the judge.

Zeke nodded to Luther who released his grip.

'My strongbox is down in the cellar. Come with me and take a look. The cupboard's bare.'

He led the way. The cellar door was still open. Taking the lamp from Zeke, Luther followed him down. Zeke, who did not trust the judge, waited at the top of the stairs.

'This is my strongbox,' said the judge. 'See? It's empty. Cleaned out. Nothing left. All gone!'

Luther yanked him aside, held the

lamp high and stared at the empty shelves as if looking could make its missing contents return.

'You got another strongbox some-where?' he snarled.

'No,' said the judge. 'That's it. I was cleaned out. I'm broke. Finished.'

There was a helpless, defeated note in the judge's voice that convinced even Luther Hayes that he was speaking the truth.

'A judge that's broke ain't no good to me,' he said and flying into a rage he lashed out. His left fist connected with the side of the judge's head like a hammer. The judge fell and did not get up. Luther kicked him in the spine then walked up the stairs to rejoin Zeke. When he got to the top, he turned and hurled the lamp at the unconscious man. It broke, oil spilled, flames fed on the oil and spread. In no time the place was a raging inferno.

'Come on!' said Zeke. 'We got to get out of here. The fire will attract attention. Soon the place will be crawling with people.'

Outside, Kelly was struggling to hold the horses that had smelled smoke.

'You get the money?' he called as he swung up into the saddle.

'No!' yelled Luther. 'But don't ask questions! Just ride!'

★ ★ ★

When no shots were fired in return, Tondu gave the order to cease fire. Leaving Sheriff O'Leary in charge, he took one of the cowboys and went looking for Daco. He found him where he had been clubbed down. He was conscious but dazed. Light, still showing at the open window, told the story.

He sent the cowboy back to O'Leary to let him know the birds had flown. He stayed a moment with his old friend who was now sitting up with his back to the wall and taking notice again. Then he climbed through the window and found Cousins still bound and gagged in the strongroom. He undid the gag and untied his hands and feet. Then, calling to the sheriff to let him know he was coming out, he opened the door.

O'Leary had already sent men to bring up the horses. They reported that Jamieson, the cowboy who'd been left in charge of them, had been overpowered and three horses had gone.

One of the cowboys said Clip was dead and Duffy was bleeding from the shoulder and weak with loss of blood.

'Get the doctor,' said O'Leary. 'This man is a witness. We'll need him for the trial.'

'And tell him to have a look at Daco,' added Tondu. 'He's round the back. He took a nasty crack on the head. Oh, and the bank manager could do with some attention. He's not used to playing rough games with big boys.'

As he spoke, there was a commotion and the horses arrived. The cowboys mounted and, led by Tondu on the black stallion, they were just shaping up to ride out when there was a shout. Holding a kerchief to his head, Daco appeared round the side of the bank.

'You ain't going without me,' he cried and made for the mustang.

'Some heads is thicker than others,' said Tondu with a grin, then added, in the same spirit, 'but be sure you keep up, you hear?'

One of the cowboys who'd fetched the horses from the corral said:

'According to Jamieson, there were three of them.'

'That figures,' said Tondu. 'Luther, Zeke and Kelly. Those odds are sure changing in our favour.'

'And they were heading west, back towards Blackmill Creek.'

Then there was a whoop and suddenly the air was full of smoke.

'Where's the fire?'

Someone, a neighbour, shouted out: 'The judge's residence!'

Tondu led the posse to the house on the edge of town where flames were already shooting fifty feet into the air. The building was already beyond saving.

'Looks like Luther's handiwork,' said

Daco. 'Before leaving town, he called on the judge, maybe to rob him, maybe to settle a score. Chances are the judge is buried under that inferno.'

One of the cowboys reported tracks in the dirt road heading west.

'Come on,' said Daco. 'What are we waiting for?'

★   ★   ★

It was Zeke who spotted the dust of a group of riders in the strengthening light. They were maybe a couple of miles off. The three men watched for a moment. There were too many to make a fight of it.

'Change of plan,' said Luther. 'We head for the river.'

His idea had been to hide up at Daco Ward's place in Green Pasture until the fuss died down and the men hunting him gave up. Zeke had said this was a bad idea: Ward would never give up and his homestead would be his first port of call. 'Good,' Luther had grunted. 'Save me the bother of looking for him. I got another reason now for wanting him dead: he put his spoke into us robbing the bank too.' But faced with the prospect of being trailed to a dead-end valley by a large posse ready to fight, he decided revenge must wait.

They did not strike out across country but stayed on the trail. They made no attempt to hide from their pursuers from whom they were concealed at intervals by folds in the landscape.

The low morning sun was already warm on their backs when what was left of the Hayes gang reined in their lathered horses and looked down at Blackmill Creek nestling in a shallow glen below them. But that sun was also high enough to glint on the surface of the Ogwy, which ran through the cluster of clapboard buildings that made up the town. The river moved fast here, fast enough to power the mill that gave the place its name. But half a mile downstream, it widened and its course was placid. Before a toll bridge wide enough to take a cart was built in the town, a ferry had connected both banks at this lower point. It wasn't used much now. Travellers, farmers and drovers found the bridge more convenient, despite the higher tolls. But it was still in occasional use. And now Luther turned off the trail and made straight for it.

'Why in tarnation,' snorted Kelly, 'did we come back here when we could have followed the railroad out of Bridgend, jumped a train and left the posse for dead?'

'Because trains don't go where we're going,' said Luther.

'And where's that?' asked Kelly.

'You'll never find out if you keep asking fool questions,' snapped Luther.

'A place called Choking Gap,' said Zeke. 'Like Luther says, it's way off the beaten track.'

'And how do we get there?' asked Kelly.

'We float,' said Luther, 'down the river.'

Esdras Higgins had been sitting on the porch of his office since sunup, waiting for trade as he did every day of his life. Business was so bad that he couldn't afford to pass up any opportunity of custom. The ferry was his living. He'd dreamed up the idea of it and he'd built it himself, here, where the river ran slow. It was a strong, flat raft made of logs. It had a handrail running round three sides for passengers to hold on to when the river was running full. The remaining side was left open. It was the side which docked at the landing jetty and embarked passengers and freight, and was just big enough to take a cart or three men and their mounts. It was operated by a horse pulling an endless rope on a rotating capstan.

Es was proud of what he had built. He had been prosperous, well known and well-respected. But since the bridge had been built, folks couldn't be bothered to come the half-mile from town to his ferry. Es hated that bridge and hardly an hour went by each day when he did not curse it. It not only ruined his business, it made him look foolish, as if he lacked the brains to look ahead and see it coming.

The sound of hoofs moving fast brought him back to reality. He got up. Three men. Horses in a sweat. Es was curious.

'Take us across,' said a growling voice. The voice belonged to a large man. 'The three of us.'

'Horses too?' said Es.

'No. Just the three of us.'

'Dollar fifty,' said Es. 'Fifty cents a head. Payment in advance.'

Luther reached his hand down his pants but instead of producing coins from his pocket, he came up with a gun.

'We want to cross now!' he said.

'You're the boss,' said Es nervously. He didn't like guns. 'Step aboard.'

The three jayhawkers unslung the money bags and stuffed them into three separate waterproof canvas sacks reluctantly supplied at gunpoint by Es Higgins. They also raided his stores for rope. When the going got rough, the sacks would keep the money and their guns dry and the rope would keep them on board. They got on to the ferry. Es untied the moorings. Luther watched as Es, still at gunpoint, unhitched the horse that turned the capstan. It didn't need to be told what to do but automatically started walking the circle it had been following for ten years. On rare occasions when Es freed it from its labours, such as taking it to the farrier in town for shoeing, he had to lean hard against it to keep it on the trail; it had forgotten how to walk in a straight line.

It wasn't the first time Es had been held up at gunpoint. He knew what he had to do. Once the ferry was in midstream, he'd halt the horse and go for the sheriff. The men wouldn't be going anywhere unless they could swim and not many in this parched country could. They'd still be there when he got back. If they were gone, they were either dead or had got across and were not a problem. The horse started turning the capstan and the ferry started moving. Es watched it move slowly out over the flat surface of the Ogwy which gave him his living, such as it was.

It had not gone more than a third of the way when Es saw the big man take a hunting knife from his belt and start cutting the hauling rope on the near side of the raft. The rope was thick but the knife must have been strong and sharp, for the rope parted and the horse turning the capstan found itself pulling slack rope. It slipped and fell on its knees.

The ferry, free to roam, made the most of the opportunity. It turned in the sluggish water then began sliding slowly downstream with the current.

Es rushed into his office for his gun. He was damned if three strangers thought they could show up, steal his ferry and get away with it. But as he came through the door, gun raised to pepper their hides, a bullet thudded into the woodwork by his head. He ducked back inside for cover.

Though the river ran slowly here, it still moved at least as fast as a man could walk. Within minutes it was out of range and Es came out to watch it go. Soon it reached the bend where the river-bed began its long, gradual descent to Funnel Gorge, where it was forced into a narrow passage between high-sided rocks and foamed mightily in its eagerness to be through and quiet again.

As his ferry rounded the bend and disappeared from sight, Es wondered if those three bandidos knew exactly what they were heading for.

16

After he'd watched his livelihood float away downstream in the direction of perdition, Esdras Higgins sat down on his porch, tilted his hat over his eyes and pushed back on two legs of his chair. He didn't move. He was thinking.

After a while, he opened his eyes and looked out at a strange sight: his landing jetty with no ferry anywhere near it.

His thinking had come to nothing. He had no idea what to do next. Maybe he should step along to the sheriff in Blackmill Creek and tell him what had happened. But what good would that do? The sheriff wasn't going to bring his ferry back.

He went on sitting there. He rolled himself a cigarette. He had just finished smoking it when he heard the sound of horses. More than three this time.

He reached for his gun. He had nothing of value left to take, except a broken-winded horse and his pride. But this time, no one was going to get the drop on him. Still, when he saw the star on the leading rider's vest, he relaxed.

Tondu, Daco and O'Leary's band of cowboys had stayed on Luther's trail, no trouble. They'd even kept him in sight most of the time until they were cut off by the last crest before the descent into Blackmill Creek. They'd ridden into town and asked if anyone had seen three men passing through. No one had, but someone suggested they could have used Es's ferry. That way they could have crossed the river without being noticed. Hardly anybody used the ferry any more. It was a shame . . .

'Morning,' said Tondu. 'You seen anything of three riders?'

'Horses in a lather?' asked Es.

'Yep.'

'A big feller in charge?'

'That's right. Did you ferry them across?'

'Yes and no,' said Es, who was beginning to enjoy being important.

'Did you or didn't you?' snapped Daco. Being roughed up by Luther in back of the bank had raised his dander and he was short on patience. He wanted Luther and wouldn't be easy till he had got even.

'See them horses?' asked Es, pointing to the animals Luther, Zeke and Kelly had left. They had stopped sweating and were grazing patiently on a patch of green that grew by the water's edge. Daco recognized his mustang and Tondu's black stallion.

'I see them,' said Tondu patiently. He saw that Es Higgins wasn't a man to be hurried.

'They didn't want the horses to go with them. They left them here. With me,' Es added brightly, for a thought had just struck him: at least he had come out of the disaster with three horses and saddles. Must be worth —

'Ever see them before?'

'Sure did. Saw two of 'em. The big

feller and his sidekick. They was here a couple of weeks back. Asking questions.'

'What questions?'

'This and that. About a place called Green Pasture and how they might get there. And about the river and what was upstream and downstream. They were mighty curious.'

'So you took the three men across?'

'Started to but they pulled a gun on me. Wouldn't pay the fifty cents a head. When they was about a third of the way over, they cut the line. Last I saw of them, they were floating down river on my ferry.'

'Stop playing games,' said Daco now plumb out of patience.

'Ain't no game,' said Es. 'Look for yourself. You see anything that looks like a ferry?'

Daco stared in disbelief.

'But it can't be,' he said. 'No one goes down the Ogwy! They'll get smashed up in the Funnel.'

'The Funnel sure can be a bitch,' said

Es, 'but the feller who cut the rope might do it. He looked as if he knew what he was about. And the ferry won't break up easy. Made her myself. Made her to last. Nope, all things considered, they got a good chance of getting through.'

'What about a couple of men in a canoe?' asked Tondu. 'You reckon they might make it through the rapids?'

Es screwed up his face and thought about it.

'Be a lot easier if the river was running fuller. If I had to, that's when I'd do it.'

'And when would that be?' asked Daco.

'Next spring,' said Es, without a smile, though he reckoned he'd just made the best joke he'd cracked all year.

'And what would you give for those men's chances if they tried it today?' said Tondu, before Daco blew his top.

Es thought again.

'If the canoe was light and they were experienced men,' he said finally, 'I'd say they'd have a chance.'

'You got a canoe?'

'Have I got a canoe? Look, mister, a man in my business has got to have a means of getting around on the river. Sure I got a canoe. More than one. Made 'em all myself.'

'Is that one moored by the jetty made for two men?'

'Nope. But I got such a boat. A sturdy little item.'

Daco slid off his horse while Tondu talked to the riders in the posse. He told them he and Daco were going after Luther but there was only room for two in the boat and only one boat. He said they were to split up, a couple to ride back to Bridgend and let O'Leary know what was going on. When the sheriff was through looking into the business of the fire at the judge's house, he'd want to be there when they caught up with Luther. The rest he told to ride with them along the river-bank. Luther would have to land somewhere sooner or later and numbers would matter. They'd take

Daco's mustang and Tondu's black stallion with them in hope of joining up with them later, downstream, as and when they could.

Es listened. When Tondu had finished, he said:

'The mustang and the black are mine. Seized to compensate for the ferry I lost.'

'They were stolen from us,' said Daco. 'You can have the nags my pardner and me were riding when we got here. It's a fair exchange.'

Es looked the horses over. Then he nodded.

'It's a deal,' he said. The horseflesh was about the same quality but the saddles were newer. 'If you're thinking of having these fellers here ride down the Ogwy, it's easier said than done. There ain't a towpath, no sir, and the trail that runs alongside the river goes through rough country. Have to make detours inland to get round some of them high banks.'

Then Es got the canoe ready and it

was time to go. As Daco and Tondu were climbing into it, Es sidled up and whined:

'Listen, mister. I just lost my ferry. I ain't counting on losing my two-man canoe as well . . . '

'Don't worry, Mr Higgins, sir,' replied Tondu. 'I have authority to say that you'll be fully compensated. The men who shanghaied your ferry are criminals on the run. When we bring them to justice, you won't lose none by it. Here, I'll sign you a receipt. Makes it official.'

After a couple of minutes of humming and hawing, for form's sake, Es let himself be persuaded.

'Got any advice on how to take the river?'

'Easy going for the first ten mile,' said Es promptly. 'Then you come to a bend. That's where it'll start getting rough. When you get into the Funnel try to keep to the right. The worst part is maybe half a mile long. The water will start running fast. Not falls exactly, more a series of ledges that go deeper on the right side. There the water's deeper too and ain't stirred up so much. You won't need to dodge so many rocks if you take that side. The current flows much faster on the left, where it's shallower. After the half mile, you'll be through the worst, but there's still plenty of white water ahead. When the banks start getting lower, you'll be just about through and the river settles down.'

'Much obliged, Mr Higgins,' said Daco, and he pushed off. He led, while Tondu paddled at his back.

When they'd gone, the cowboys who'd ridden with them from Bridgend took off in a cloud of dust.

As it settled, Esdras Higgins sat down in the chair on his porch and wondered how much his newly acquired horse-flesh was worth, with and without saddles. Probably a lot more than what he could earn in a year running his ferry across the Ogwy. So it hadn't been too bad a day after all.

For the first few miles, Daco and Tondu paddled hard down the calm highway of slowly moving water. The ferry that floated couldn't go faster than the current, so two men paddling a canoe would make much better time. Daco had hopes of catching Luther before he got to the bend that marked the start of the Funnel. But it was a tall order, given the start the bandidos had on them.

At first, they kept seeing O'Leary's cowboys tagging them along the right-hand bank of the river. The going was flat and easy. But at intervals rocky outcrops drove the riders inland where they lost ground. And when the banks began to rise, Daco and Tondu lost sight of them for long stretches. Finally, they lost contact altogether.

Ahead, the horizon was formed by the low line of the Bendigo Hills which was broken by a V-shaped notch. Daco assumed that the 'V' was the Funnel through which the Ogwy would squeeze itself in its long journey down to the Plains. Eventually Tondu pointed ahead.

'There's the bend the ferryman said was the start of the Funnel. Keep to the right!'

The warning wasn't needed, for already they could both feel the pull of the river. They were no longer skimming over its surface, piggy-backing on its current, but fighting currents that bounced off the banks and threatened to take them where they didn't want to go, towards surging eddies and whirlpools stirred up by boulders on the river-bed, which they didn't see until it was nearly too late.

Their arms started to ache with the effort of keeping the boat straight and closer to the right bank than the left. Their speed increased and they were soon soaked by spray thrown up by the foaming water. But this was nothing to what they had to face, for not fifty yards ahead, on each side of the now roaring river, rose almost vertical cliffs of sheer rock.

They were about to enter the Funnel.

For the first ten miles of slack water, Luther had chafed at the slowness of their progress. He couldn't make the ferry go faster and he couldn't keep it straight. They kept turning in circles helplessly as the current took them. Then there was Kelly who kept asking tomfool questions about where they were going and when would there be a divvying up of the loot. Since there was nothing else to do, he was all for counting the money there and then. In the end, Luther pulled out his gun and said he'd blow his head off if he didn't shut up.

He knew the river. Maybe a month before, he and his gang had followed the Ogwy on their way to find Ward in Green Pasture. Outfits like his never used public trails unless they had to. They kept out of sight and remembered the routes they took, the cover it offered, places for an ambush, access to water, which might be useful if ever they came back that way. Luther and Zeke had a good idea of what lay ahead once they got round the bend.

As soon as the banks started to rise and the current picked up speed, he cut a length of the ferryman's rope, tied his money bag securely around his chest and lashed himself to the handrail. He told the others to do the same. When they entered the Funnel, they'd have no means of controlling the ferry, which would be tossed around like a cork in the churning water. If they didn't secure themselves, they'd be thrown off the way a stubborn bronco can throw even the handiest of horse-breakers.

And then the roar of the water made further speech impossible.

The ferry was taken by a giant hand and thrown around. Sheer, smooth walls of glistening, moss-covered rock rushed past at tremendous speed and the three men felt the timbers under them ripple as they were buffeted by surging waves of water. There were bone-jarring jolts when they snagged on the rocky bed of the channel. The current kept pulling them to the left where the water was shallower and raced faster. The ferry shuddered as they smashed against some hidden obstacle and was turned this way and that until they felt dizzy. Water broke constantly over them, making it almost impossible to breathe. At times they were submerged for what seemed minutes on end and they felt their lungs would burst.

And then the worst of their mad ride on their surging, frantic helter-skelter was over. The ferry had held together. It straightened and moved into a stretch of white water. But if they were clear of the Funnel, they weren't safe yet. They'd made a hundred yards down the rapids when Zeke pointed to the spray rising ahead of them. Luther saw the danger at the same time. A large wedge of rock had split from the side of the channel where it had been weakened by spring floods. It blocked half the channel. Too large to be pushed out of the way by the current, it stood like a lion in their path. It sat in a boiling cauldron of raging water, which, frustrated in its onward flow, backed up, turned on itself then charged back into the swirling vortex like a drunk diving back into a brawl.

The ferry, still moving fast, smashed squarely into the obstacle. The bolts and braces holding the timbers snapped and the whole structure disintegrated like spilled matchsticks. Luther was thrown into the water where the undertow started dragging him down. But the length of rail he had lashed himself to caught on a rock and jerked him back to the surface. As he gasped for air, he saw Zeke, also borne up by the spar he was tied to, being carried along furiously by the torrent. Then he too was past the rock and within minutes the stretch of white water stopped being angry and changed into what, in comparison, seemed like a mill pond.

Luther, bruised and exhausted, paddled his way somehow to a low, sandy beach and pulled himself onto it. Zeke was already there, on his back, gasping, staring up at sky and clouds he'd thought he'd never see again. Luther was the first to recover. He sat up and cut the rope which attached him to the spar that had saved his life. He freed the sack which held the money and opened it: the money was dry; so was his gun.

'What happened to Kelly?' said Zeke, struggling on to one elbow.

Luther didn't answer. He was staring at a dead tree which had been washed down with the flood and had fetched up on the opposite bank of the river. Caught in its branches was a body of what, only minutes before, had been a man. It had been horribly mauled, flayed as if it had been sanded down by a cheese grater. It must have been held under the water and been repeatedly battered against sharp rocks by frenzied currents. One arm was missing and the head was twisted at an unnatural angle. The face was turned towards them. There was no expression on it. The clothes had been mostly torn off, but there was enough of them and of the body left to confirm that it was John Kelly.

There was no sign of his money bag.

'Damn Kelly to hell!' muttered Luther. 'He was always a useless man.'

Zeke cut himself out of his harness of ropes and spars and felt his arms and legs and ribs. He ached but he didn't think he'd been seriously hurt.

'You know, Luther,' he said, 'you're a cold-hearted son of a bitch. How long we been together? More than twenty years and in all that time I never heard you say a good word about anybody. I don't think you got feelings. I reckon they left them out when you were born.'

'Cut that out, nobody's interested. Get across there and check that Kelly's money bag is really gone.'

'Why don't you go yourself, Luther?'

'Because I'm ordering you to.'

'Listen, big man, you got a big mouth and big fists but you're not so big. You know, you're really very stupid. You

213

never think before you act because you got no brains. We've pulled a lot of jobs together, you and me. But who was it always saw the angles, made the plan work, looked after the practical details? Me! Without me, you're nothing. So if you're so anxious to know if Kelly's money bag is tied to his leg or floating down this damned river that nearly killed the both of us, go see for yourself. I just stopped obeying stupid orders.'

Zeke stood and turned his back on Luther Hayes and stared across the river to get a clearer sight of Kelly's mangled body.

As the words sank in, Luther's head filled with rage. No brains? This from a man who would have been nothing without the protection he, Luther Hayes, boss man of the Hayes gang, had given him! Zeke was a bendy reed. He did all right as long as he was obeying orders. He needed a leader. Luther was a leader. No one should talk to his leader that way.

He looked at Zeke's back. He looked

at Zeke's sack. Zeke hadn't earned that money. He had no right to it. Next thing he'd be asking for half shares. Maybe more.

Luther couldn't allow that.

He raised his gun and pulled the trigger.

The bullet got Zeke in the middle of the back.

At such close range, the impact of the shot knocked him clean off his feet. He ended up stretched out flat on the damp sand. He died with his boots on and his eyes wide open.

Zeke Goodwin lay staring across the river at John Kelly.

John Kelly stared back.

17

Neither Tondu nor Daco had any idea how bad riding the Funnel would be. The smell of fear, madness and death hung everywhere. It got in their nostrils, their lungs and filled their heads.

The moment they were sucked between the sheer sides that shut out the light and painted gloom over the heaving, racing mass of water, they were fighting for their lives.

Heaving mounds of snarling green water reared up at them like dangerous beasts which changed shape menacingly. Rocky overhangs leaned down on them, threatening to push them under. Spray like driving rain drenched them within seconds. It all kept coming, getting bigger, angrier. Nothing was still for a moment. Every split second called for a response. Sitting in the front of the canoe, Daco watched for the submerged, jagged teeth of the ledges Es Higgins had talked about. He dug his paddle deep in the water and hauled the boat away from them only to find he had succeeded in pointing the bow at another rock. There was no time to warn Tondu, but the big man was just as quick and sharp-eyed and straightened up the boat by sheer muscle power.

But Es had given them useful advice. The water was deeper on the right side of the channel and the clearance that much greater. They slid over the writhing water and the rock below them didn't have the reach to tear out the bottom of the boat.

Daco's body ached with the strain but gradually he began to believe they would come out of the experience alive. He kept one eye open for signs of the ferry, but he saw nothing. Not that he really expected to. If Luther had come to grief the debris would have been flushed far away by now.

It was Tondu who first saw the great

wedge of cliff-face slip, which stuck out half way across the width of the white-water race.

'Left!' he shouted. 'Go left!'

Daco saw it too and dug his paddle deep, held it there until, between them, the nose of the boat started to come round. They sped past the fallen rock with inches to spare. Almost at once the river started to slow. They began losing speed and regained control. Once past the white water, the river widened again and flowed more smoothly. They felt safe enough to let themselves be taken by the current. They flopped over their paddles, utterly spent, their breath coming in great, agonizing gasps.

Tondu, first to recover, saw splintered spars of the raft littering both sides of the river. With a few strokes of his paddle, he steered the boat to a place on a bend where the right bank dropped to form a small beach. They were through the low line of the Bendigo Hills and the land here stretched away on both sides in gentle, welcoming undulations.

By the time Daco recovered, Tondu had seen Kelly spread-eagled on his tree on the other side of the water and, a few yards downstream, he found Zeke.

'They must have smashed into that rock fall,' said Tondu. 'It broke them up.'

'It's hard it believe how anyone who fell into that devil's cauldron could have come out of it alive,' said Daco.

Then he looked round and reached for his gun.

'Any sign of Luther?' he asked. 'If he made it, he could have us in his sights.'

'Don't think so,' said Tondu. 'The river did for Kelly but Zeke's got a big bullet hole in his back. Must have been Luther. He'll be long gone.'

'Why would he shoot Zeke? He needed Zeke. Zeke was the one with brains.'

'Maybe Luther wanted all the money, including Zeke's share. Who knows why thieves fall out?'

'Any way of telling which way he

went?' asked Daco.

They started looking for tracks.

★   ★   ★

Luther shouldered both remaining money bags and climbed the river-bank. To his right were the Bendigo Hills, so he struck off left, following a diagonal route that took him south-east, away from the river. Luther knew exactly where he was going.

He knew the terrain hereabouts. After the War, he'd built up his band of mavericks and ranged far and wide over the whole of Colorado. His jaywalkers had even operated in this neck of the woods and it was then that he'd first heard talk of Choking Gap, sometimes known as Tagu Gap. The Ogwy Indians had believed it was the sacred home of gods who kept their enemies out by poisoning the air and choking them. The word tagu was Ogwy for 'choke'.

Luther's boys had pulled off a few jobs in Ogmore County. They'd stopped a stage and robbed a train outside Bridg-end and needed a safe place to stash the loot. Zeke got interested in Choking Gap and liked what he heard. It was what they were looking for, a deserted gulch with natural defences. It was safer than any bank.

He asked around and located Choking Gap. It was in an area where the land rose in a whole series of gulches, some small, some big. The entrance was through a break in the side of a low bluff, hidden by a fold of rock. It was a narrow funnel, like the neck of a bottle, just wide enough for a single mounted rider to get through at a time, which made it easy for a couple of men to defend it indefinitely. Once through the gap, Zeke found a dry water course which descended, gently at first and then steeply, down an almost sheer-sided bowl, maybe a quarter of a mile across. The bottom of the bowl usually started the day wrapped in dank morning mist but this was quickly burned off by the sun to reveal a morass of evil-smelling black sludge, which bubbled and belched like thick soup simmering in a pot. It was the smell of rotten rankness and it made the air too heavy to escape until a build-up raised it high enough for the winds on the higher slopes to blow it away. That air killed everything that breathed. Despite the reputation of Choking Gap and the bleached bones of dead animals littering the thin rim of rock that circled the lethal swamp, Zeke reckoned he could get round it. He covered his face with his neckerchief, wrapped a bandanna around his horse's nostrils and rode round the quagmire as fast as he could.

Man and animal came to no harm.

On the further side, a second water course, also dry at that season, led up to a narrow valley riddled with caves. Luther followed him through and picked one out. Thereafter he and his gang used the place to stash what they had stolen.

It was for Choking Gap that Luther was now headed.

He felt good. He was rich. His gang

were all dead or in custody. He was the only man in the world who knew about treasure valley. He was the sole survivor and he intended to claim the spoils. He was pushing fifty, pushing his luck. Maybe it was time to hang up his gun.

But he needed to move fast. He knew Ward wouldn't give up, and he wasn't far behind. He'd find the remains of the ferry and pick up his trail. Ward! He remembered the moment he'd seen him that day in Blackmill Creek. He'd never expected to see him again! And there he was, large as life, having a drink, buying supplies, as if he'd never sent anyone to jail for thirty years. He and Zeke asked around, found out where his place was, rode out and shot that dumb wife of his who wouldn't do what she was told. Luther's hand strayed to his gun. He imagined having half a chance, that's all he asked for, a quarter chance of a shot at Ward. By God, he'd make it tell!

Cresting a rise, he was jerked back to the present. Ahead of him was a small-holding in a hollow. A settler in a check shirt was ploughing a fenced-off field. Luther changed course. From the fence, he called to the man who finished his furrow before walking across to him.

When the farmer was five yards from him, Luther produced his gun and shot him in the head.

The man's wife ran out of the house when she heard the shot.

'Where d'you keep the horse?' barked Luther. 'In that barn?'

The woman, terrified, nodded.

'Get me some provisions together. Bacon, biscuit, coffee.'

The woman did not move. She was paralyzed by shock and fear.

'Now!! Don't keep me waiting!' he thundered.

Luther walked the horse out of the stable then returned for the battered saddle which he belted under the animal's belly. He hung his money bags from the pommel. To them he added the sack of provisions the woman tremblingly gave him and cantered off.

The woman, the world's newest

widow, ran across the field to where her man lay inert in a furrow.

★　★　★

Luther had gone to a lot of trouble to hide his tracks. He'd waded down the river in the shallow water's edge for a quarter of a mile before climbing on to the bank and heading off. By the time Tondu found his trail, Frenchy Durand had arrived with the horses.

Before they set off in pursuit of Luther, they laid the canoe over Zeke to protect it from scavengers. Later, they'd send a party to bury the body. There was nothing they could do for Kelly who was unreachable in his tree on the far bank.

Luther's trail was clear enough to give the general direction he had taken. At intervals, it disappeared, for he was wily enough to use stretches of gravel and bare rock wherever he could, to throw his pursuers off the scent or at least delay them. Boots leave few tracks on shale and none on rock.

Darkness was falling when they reached the farm where Luther had killed a man and stolen a horse.

The farmer's wife was distraught and it took some time to get the story out of her. The news wasn't good: Luther on a horse would now be moving faster. Moreover, it was dark and there was not light enough to follow his trail by. They bedded down for the night. Tondu and Daco slept like dead men but were up at first light and eager to be off.

All day they moved on as fast as they could. Ahead was a second line of hills which at first were purple in the hazy distance. By early afternoon, a man with keen eyes could see that they were pleasantly wooded. But whatever they looked like, it was where Luther was heading.

* * *

Luther trotted his horse along the level shelf that led to the fold of rock that disguised the entrance to Choking Gap.

But he did not stop when he reached it. He rode past it until he got to a stretch of gravel. He turned, rode back, walked his horse through the narrow gap and tethered it in a bush. He snapped a branch off the bush, returned through the narrow cleft and brushed away all trace of the tracks he had left as he returned from the gravel patch. It now looked as if he had ridden past Choking Gap onto the gravel where his trail petered out.

He unhitched his horse, mounted and rode down to the quagmire. He covered his nose and mouth, wound a cloth around his horse's face and rode briskly round the rim. On the opposite side, he followed the dry water course to the cave where the loot was hidden. It was still there.

He added the contents of the two bags to the heap, sat back and looked at his money. All his!

When it started to grow dark, he made a fire and cooked supper for himself.

He made no attempt to hide his

smoke; no one was going to find him in Choking Gap.

He curled up in his blanket and slept the sleep of the wicked.

* * *

Daco, Frenchy and a couple of the cowboys rode slowly along the level terrace Luther's tracks had led them to, their eyes fixed on the ground, looking for some trace of the passage of a horse: a stone newly turned or shale scuffed where a hoof had kicked it up.

'His tracks stop here,' Daco sang out to Tondu who had lingered on a natural shelf and was studying the rocky face of a low bluff. His eye had been caught by the way the sun struck what appeared to be unbroken rock face. Divided vertically by an invisible line, one section seemed darker than the next. He took a closer look and found a concealed cleft which turned into a narrow gap just wide enough to allow a mounted rider to push through. When he saw grass flattened at intervals and broken twigs at shoulder height, he knew he had found Luther's trail.

He called to Daco who joined him with the others. They passed though the cleft one by one then together they rode down the dried-up water course until they saw the bowl of evil-smelling swamp. Tondu reined the party in. Even from there, they felt it in their nostrils, they could taste it in the back of their throats. They turned and retreated up the slope until the air was sweet again.

'I heard of this place,' said Daco, 'but I never knew it really existed. The Ogwy called it Choking Gap on account of the air being bad. It comes off that quagmire.'

Daco looked up and ran his eyes over the sheer upper slopes of the bowl.

'There must be some way of getting past it. The Ogwy did. So has Luther. Maybe there's a trail higher up . . . ?'

But the nearest thing to a trail in sight was the narrow track running round the rim of the bowl itself. It was strewn with fallen rocks and animal bones and hadn't been in regular use for years. Yet even from this height, Daco could make out hoof marks in the dust. A horse had ridden along it very recently.

'You're right,' said Tondu. 'That's the way Luther went. He's gone to ground on the far side of the bowl.'

'Listen, Tondu,' said Daco. 'I know you've been after Luther a long time. But I got first claim on him. He shot Ginny, robbed Tom of a mother. He's mine! He owes me and I'm going to make him pay. It's something I got to do.'

Tondu was about to argue when he saw the fire in Daco's eye.

'Have it your way, friend,' he said. 'I reckon you're top of the list.'

'Here's the way of it,' said Daco. 'You and the boys stay here. I'll go round the swamp and flush him out. If I don't come back inside a couple of hours, he's yours. If the Ogwy set such store by the front way into their sacred place, there sure as teeth won't be a back way out. Luther ain't going anywhere. If he wants to get out of here, he'll have to come this way. That'll be your chance for a tilt at him.'

As he talked, Daco improvised protective masks for himself and his horse.

'Go get him!' called Tondu as Daco rode down to the quagmire.

He took the mustang round it at a fast canter. When he reached the other side, he stopped, waved his hat to show that the precautions had worked and rode on.

He hadn't gone far when he got the acrid tang of wood smoke in his nostrils. Then he heard a horse neigh. He dismounted and proceeded on foot. He eased the six-gun from his belt. He doubted if Luther was expecting visitors — his hideaway was much too well-hidden for a surprise raid — but Daco did not underestimate the man. He was a rat and he was tough. But any sort of rat, tough or not, fights when cornered.

Treading carefully through the under-brush, Daco stopped at a boulder and peered round it.

Not twenty yards away, Luther Hayes was sitting by a camp-fire on a round boulder outside the mouth of a cave. His gun-belt hung from a snag on the rocky wall. But a Winchester was propped within reach against a make-shift table made of heaped stones. On the table were bags. The bags looked round and plump. Daco was sure they weren't full of apples.

Luther was taking stock of his loot.

Daco stepped from behind his rock and shot Luther's hat off his head.

Luther turned fast, half stood, reached for his holster as he rose and then, realizing he wasn't carrying a gun, sat down again.

'Well, well! If it's not Sergeant Ward!' he said. 'You're proving to be like something I trod in and jest cain't get off my boot!'

Daco looked at him.

'It's been a long time since we stood

face to face like this, Corporal,' he said, 'just the two of us. Pity Zeke ain't here. I always enjoyed his conversation more than yours. But he's still on that river-bank, with a hole in his back. How come he died that way, Luther? I never figured you for a backshooter.'

Luther shrugged.

'But I was forgetting,' Daco went on. 'You shoot women in the back too, don't you, big man.'

Luther looked up and grinned.

'So that's what this is all about! You're sore because I shot your woman!'

'You're damn right, Luther, and I'm going to show you just how sore I am.'

Shooting was for mad dogs. Mad dogs didn't know what they were doing. Luther did. Shooting was too good for him. Daco threw down his gun and squared up.

Luther's face lit up. He had four, five inches reach and twenty pounds on Daco. He could handle him. Easy. That time round the back of the bank Ward had been lucky. He stood up, bunched his fists and went for Daco at a run.

Daco dodged his first wild swing and got in close with a savage right to the heart and a looping left which split his opponent's eyebrow. Blood flowed down Luther's cheek and over the front of his shirt. He stopped for a moment in surprise, wiped the blood out of his eye, and charged again with a roar, but his flailing fists found only empty air. In his eagerness, he overbalanced again and Daco got in with a combination of straight rights and crunching lefts which made Luther shake his head to clear it. Seizing his chance, Daco darted in again, landing heavily again with both hands.

'Stand your ground, Ward,' Luther spluttered. 'What are you? A dancing man?'

Daco was still breathing easy. In the old days, when he fought bare-knuckle for money at fairgrounds and rodeos, he'd faced many opponents like Luther. Big and clumsy they were, but also dangerous. They soaked up punishment. They had granite jaws and thick bony heads. He was taking nothing for granted. Anyway, he was in no hurry. He'd waited a long time for the chance to have a crack at the big man. The bigger the beating he handed out, the longer it took, the happier he would be. For Ginny's sake.

Warier now, Luther began to circle, making his man retreat before him, trying to back him into corners he couldn't dance out of. But Daco wouldn't be pinned down and kept slipping his opponent's guard with punches to head and body which made Luther grunt but did not stop him.

So far, Daco was virtually unmarked while Luther's face was a mass of cuts. There was a gash in his right cheek, exposing bone, and his lower lip was deeply split. His heavy breathing suggested that his nose was broken. But Luther was a brawler and did not give up easy. Switching his attack, he sank into a crouch and tried to rush Daco and wrestle him to the ground. Daco stepped back, avoided his lunge but as he did so trod on a stone which gave under his foot. He went down. Luther was on him at once, like a ravening wolf. He stood over him and kicked him in the ribs, on the arms, in the head, until Daco's head rang.

Bracing himself, he caught the next boot Luther aimed at his ribs and twisted hard. Luther staggered and ended up on all fours. Daco was on his feet before Luther could get up. When he did, he had a rock in his hand. He rushed Daco again and waved his loaded fist in his face. Daco danced away. Luther stopped and grinned, though he was blowing hard.

'I watched her, Ward,' he said indistinctly through his split lips. 'I let her run till she was nearly at the cow byre, nearly safe. Then I let her have it!'

He paused, then cocking his thumb as though it was a gun, he added: '*Bang!*'

If his plan was to make Daco so mad he would come on to him and get careless, he was only half right. He got mad to be sure: he came on to Luther with one thing in mind — to beat him to a pulp. But he stayed cool, clinical, in control of himself and the fight. He came in low with an uppercut that started somewhere around Luther's knees and ended a split second later on the point of his chin. The big man staggered and dropped his guard. Daco followed up with a series of heavy left jabs followed by a roundhouse right, which landed on Luther's left jaw. He went down. As he got up, Daco went for him with all the cold venom of his anger and the power of his grief for Ginny.

Three times Luther got up and three times Daco cut him to pieces until the big man couldn't see, couldn't hold his fists up, couldn't think because his brains were scrambled.

With the man who'd killed his wife in cold blood lying in a groaning, bleeding mess in front of him, Daco retrieved his gun. Standing over him, he aimed it at his head.

Then he holstered it.

'I ain't going to kill you, Luther. There's no point in starting something I can't ever finish. Kill one rat and another steps up to the plate to take his place. There's too many of them for one man to kill. Best thing is for the hate to stop here. So long, little big man. I leave the loot to you. Enjoy it while you can.'

He found the mustang, swung into the saddle and cantered back the way he'd come.

★   ★   ★

Luther sat up. His head throbbed. He couldn't see much until he wiped the blood out of his eyes. The movement told him his jaw was broken. He wondered dazedly how he'd got into this state. Then he remembered.

Ward!

He looked round. No one. He got on to his hands and knees and waited for his head to stop spinning. As he stood up, fury flared, reviving him like a shot of rye whiskey. No one got the better of Luther Hayes! He reached for his Winchester and started along the trail leading to the choking bowl. Twice he fell and twice he got up. He felt his strength return. By the time he got near the bowl of sludge he was breathing hard but his body was doing what he told it to. The air wasn't making it any easier. It was bad here. He coughed. His head cleared. He stepped out on the rim and looked up.

High on the opposite side was a bunch of riders. A star glinted on the chest of one of the men. Then, maybe thirty feet below them, he saw a lone rider making his way up.

Ward!

He raised the Winchester and took aim. His arm was steady, he had his man in his sights, the range was right. It was a clear shot. Easy!

He pulled the trigger.

★ ★ ★

Daco heard Tondu call a warning just before the world erupted round him. He was lifted out of the saddle and dumped unceremoniously on his back. The mustang was knocked off its feet and rolled down the slope until it was brought up short in a patch of brush. Tondu's horse reared but he managed to stay in control while Frenchy and several of the cowboys were thrown.

The noise of the explosion went on reverberating round the bowl like summer thunder for several minutes. When it stopped, the silence was deafening.

Daco, ears still ringing, climbed up to where Tondu was waiting.

'What happened?' he said.

'Luther. He followed you. The damn fool stood on the rim of the bowl and took a shot at you. The shot sparked the explosion.'

'What explosion?'

'The sludge in the bowl gives off marsh gas. That's the reason why the air is bad. It's the same as the fire-damp they get in mines. It's deadly. That's why the Ogwy called this place Choking Gap. You don't breathe it and you don't want to be around either when it meets a spark. Fire-damp and sparks just don't get on.'

'And Luther?'

'Take a look. That scorched patch down there, that's what's left of him: burned to a crisp.'

'So it's over,' said Daco. 'Time to go home.'

'What about the loot?'

'Leave it to Frenchy and the boys,' said Daco. 'They can take it back to O'Leary. He'll know what to do about it. Me, I'm heading for Blackmill Creek to get my boy. We'll be going back to Green Pasture and start again. It's what Ginny would have wanted. Say, there'd be room for you too if you're tired of playing marshal.'

'You know, Daco, I might just take you up on that.'

Soon, they had all gone, and Choking Gap went back to sleep.

We do hope that you have enjoyed
reading this large print book.

Did you know that all of our titles
are available for purchase?

We publish a wide range of high
quality large print books including:
Romances, Mysteries, Classics
General Fiction
Non Fiction and Westerns

Special interest titles available in
large print are:
The Little Oxford Dictionary
Music Book, Song Book
Hymn Book, Service Book

Also available from us courtesy of
Oxford University Press:
Young Readers' Dictionary
(large print edition)
Young Readers' Thesaurus
(large print edition)

For further information or a free
brochure, please contact us at:
Ulverscroft Large Print Books Ltd.,
The Green, Bradgate Road, Anstey,
Leicester, LE7 7FU, England.
Tel: (00 44) **0116 236 4325**
Fax: (00 44) **0116 234 0205**

RETURN TO TATANKA CROSSING

Will DuRey

The war has been over for two years and Charlie Jefferson is returning home to a changed place. Neighbourliness has been replaced by greed and hostility; the cluster of buildings around Sam Flint's trading post has developed into a small township where gun-carrying saddletramps congregate; and a man called Brent Deacon is forging an empire at the expense of the original settlers. When Charlie interferes on behalf of Lars Svensson, accused of murder, it brings him into direct conflict with the dangerous Deacon . . .

GALLOWS BOUND

Ben Coady

Having hunted down notorious outlaw Frank Cuskin, Marshal Abe Ryan's problems are only just beginning. Lack of sleep, the desert, Indians, Cuskin's polecat kin, thirst and exhaustion make it ever more likely that Ryan's mission will end in failure. When Cuskin gets the upper hand and leaves him for dead, a lesser man than Ryan would have abandoned the task. But Ryan is not a lesser man, and he will use every weapon in his arsenal to deliver the killer to the gallows . . .

A MAN CALLED LAWLESS

Steve Hayes

The promise of well-paid work draws the man called Lawless to Deming, New Mexico. But when he discovers the nature of the job, he decides to pass. Fate, however, has other ideas. Within minutes of his arrival in town, he is forced to kill three hired guns, putting him at odds with the local law. And when his would-be employer is kidnapped by Mexican bandits, Lawless has no choice but to cross the border and rescue her . . .

RISING RED

Caleb Rand

US Marshal Will Ritter is used to hauling outlaws in front of a judge but this is different: Theodore Pond was once a friend. Ritter is to transport him across miles of wild territory to stand trial for murder. When the prisoner and his cohorts try to break free, Will's problems really begin. Finding himself both at the mercy of his prisoners, and the moving target of a ruthless posse, this is one journey he will be lucky to finish alive.

DOMINGO'S TRAIL

Greg Mitchell

Vicious Mexican bandit, Estrada, is holding an American to ransom in the Sabinas Valley; he has arranged for two different expeditions to come and shower him with gold in return for a safe release. But a mysterious Mexican named Domingo appears, warning that the captive is dead and that Estrada means to slaughter them all. With the combined ransom parties now joined in their mission, they are ready for bloody battle. Can Domingo's advice be trusted? And will all who follow his perilous trail survive?